I0831743

The Barders

Vol. 1

May Tranparency Be Our Currency

The Barders

Front cover and logo image by Artist, Tristan Bradshaw

Book design by Designer, Joshua Robertson

Printed in the United States of America.
First printing edition 2025.

@The.Barders.Exchange

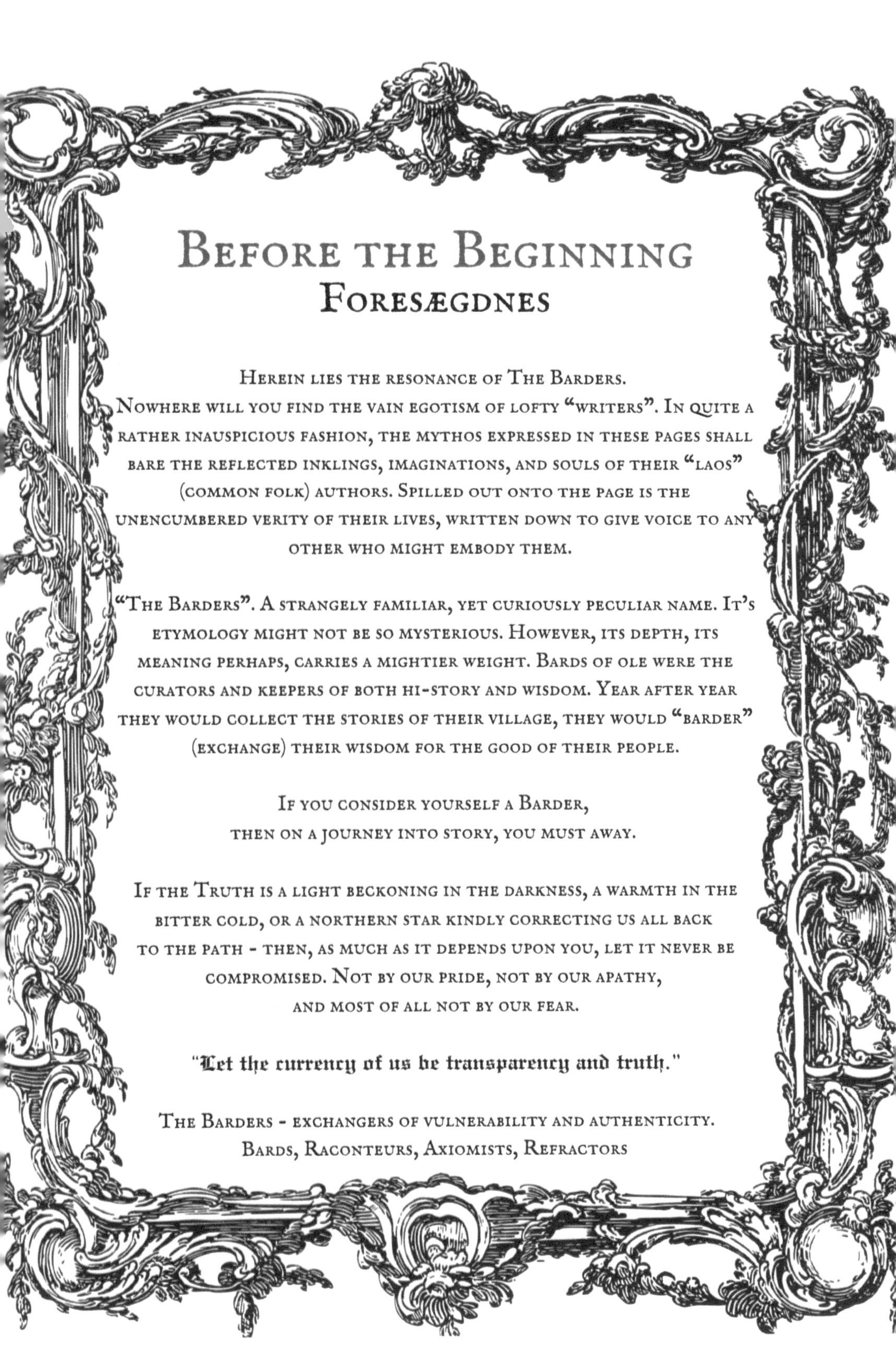

Before the Beginning
Foresægdnes

Herein lies the resonance of The Barders.
Nowhere will you find the vain egotism of lofty "writers". In quite a rather inauspicious fashion, the mythos expressed in these pages shall bare the reflected inklings, imaginations, and souls of their "laos" (common folk) authors. Spilled out onto the page is the unencumbered verity of their lives, written down to give voice to any other who might embody them.

"The Barders". A strangely familiar, yet curiously peculiar name. It's etymology might not be so mysterious. However, its depth, its meaning perhaps, carries a mightier weight. Bards of ole were the curators and keepers of both hi-story and wisdom. Year after year they would collect the stories of their village, they would "barder" (exchange) their wisdom for the good of their people.

If you consider yourself a Barder,
then on a journey into story, you must away.

If the Truth is a light beckoning in the darkness, a warmth in the bitter cold, or a northern star kindly correcting us all back to the path - then, as much as it depends upon you, let it never be compromised. Not by our pride, not by our apathy, and most of all not by our fear.

"Let the currency of us be transparency and truth."

The Barders - exchangers of vulnerability and authenticity.
Bards, Raconteurs, Axiomists, Refractors

Welcome

For as long as people have sat around fires or pushed their chairs together after a long day, we've shared stories. This book—The Barders: Vol 1—comes from that same simple tradition. It's an anthology written by regular folks: carpenters, firefighters, musicians, some businesspeople, a couple of industrial hands. None of us are professional writers. For several, this is the first story, wrought from within them, that they've ever put on a page. But we decided that wasn't a good enough reason not to try.

We wanted to show that storytelling isn't exclusive to "expertise". You have stories in you, too. Things you've lived through, things you've imagined, things you've wondered late at night. That's really how the name "The Barders" came about. It's a blend of the old bards—those wandering tellers of tales—and the idea of bartering: trading truth, swapping insight, offering pieces of ourselves. Anyone can take up that mantle. Anyone can become a "Barder."

If you're reading this, consider it a nudge. If we could do it, you certainly can. Gather a few people from your world—friends, neighbors, the quiet guy who always thinks deeply before he speaks—and just begin. Meet in your living room or around a fire pit. Ask each other what stories are sitting beneath the surface. You don't need fancy language or a degree in literature. You just need some honesty, inspiration, and a willingness to go digging.

That digging, though... it's not always easy. Every person has a kind of inner mythos, a story that explains who they are and how they got here. But pulling that story into the light takes courage. We learned quickly that you have to move past pride and past the instinct to hide. You have to be willing to be vulnerable, and to let others be vulnerable with you. It's uncomfortable at times —no point pretending otherwise—but it's also strangely freeing.

Most of our own stories grew out of nights spent talking around firelight or passing plates of food back and forth at someone's kitchen table.

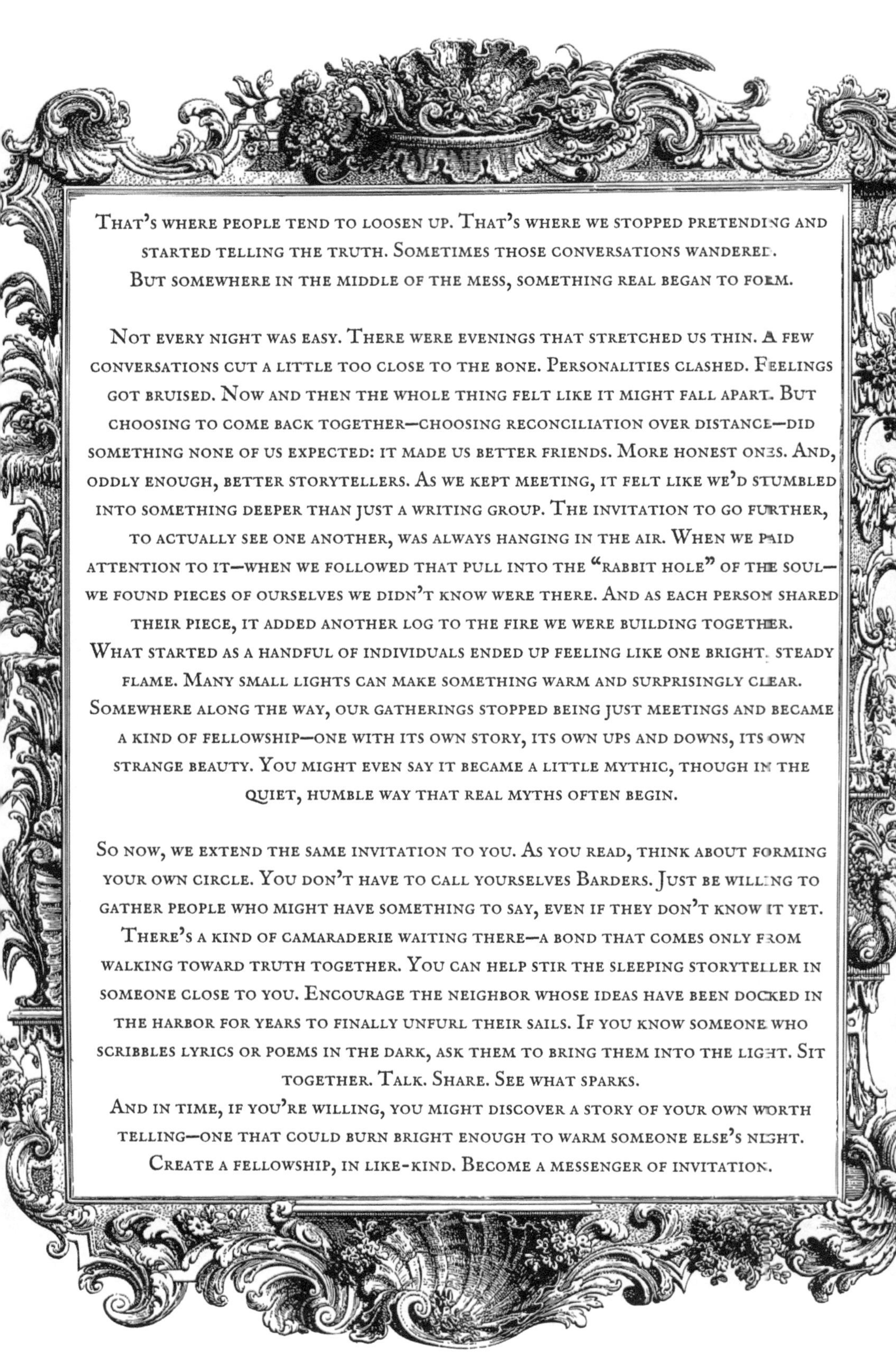

That's where people tend to loosen up. That's where we stopped pretending and started telling the truth. Sometimes those conversations wandered. But somewhere in the middle of the mess, something real began to form.

Not every night was easy. There were evenings that stretched us thin. A few conversations cut a little too close to the bone. Personalities clashed. Feelings got bruised. Now and then the whole thing felt like it might fall apart. But choosing to come back together—choosing reconciliation over distance—did something none of us expected: it made us better friends. More honest ones. And, oddly enough, better storytellers. As we kept meeting, it felt like we'd stumbled into something deeper than just a writing group. The invitation to go further, to actually see one another, was always hanging in the air. When we paid attention to it—when we followed that pull into the "rabbit hole" of the soul—we found pieces of ourselves we didn't know were there. And as each person shared their piece, it added another log to the fire we were building together. What started as a handful of individuals ended up feeling like one bright, steady flame. Many small lights can make something warm and surprisingly clear. Somewhere along the way, our gatherings stopped being just meetings and became a kind of fellowship—one with its own story, its own ups and downs, its own strange beauty. You might even say it became a little mythic, though in the quiet, humble way that real myths often begin.

So now, we extend the same invitation to you. As you read, think about forming your own circle. You don't have to call yourselves Barders. Just be willing to gather people who might have something to say, even if they don't know it yet. There's a kind of camaraderie waiting there—a bond that comes only from walking toward truth together. You can help stir the sleeping storyteller in someone close to you. Encourage the neighbor whose ideas have been docked in the harbor for years to finally unfurl their sails. If you know someone who scribbles lyrics or poems in the dark, ask them to bring them into the light. Sit together. Talk. Share. See what sparks.

And in time, if you're willing, you might discover a story of your own worth telling—one that could burn bright enough to warm someone else's night.

Create a fellowship, in like-kind. Become a messenger of invitation.

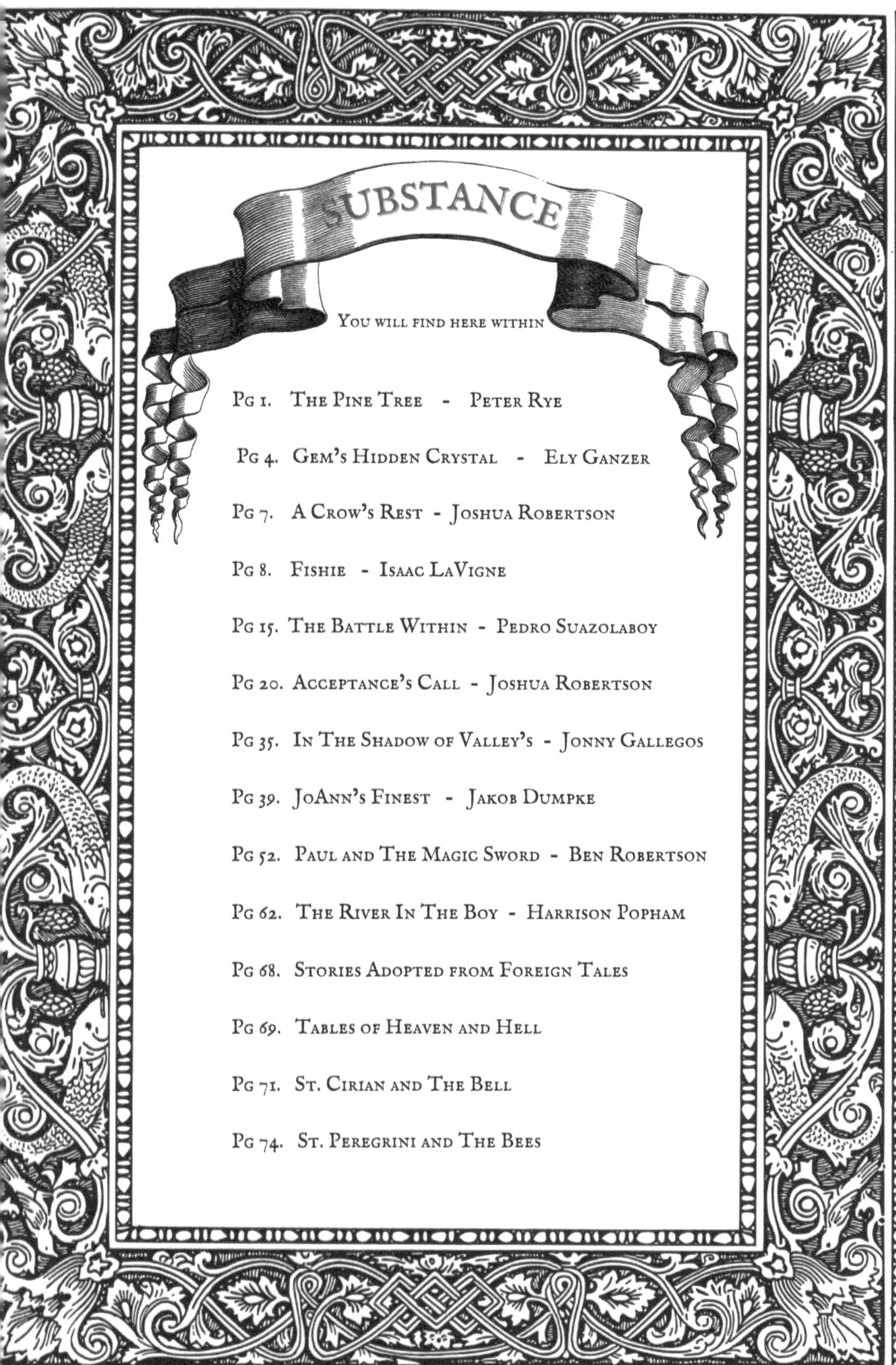

SUBSTANCE

You will find here within

The Pine Tree

by: Peter Rye

Once upon a time, in an old growth forest, there was a pine tree. His cone had fallen to the ground during a forest fire years ago, blown down from his family's tree, by the wind and smoke and flames. His seed eventually settled in soil yards away, across the creek, and he grew up amongst a grove of hardwoods, who were different from him. Having taken root, he eventually became a loblolly sapling.

Season after season, the pine tree grew, and grew tall. But, he began to notice something about himself: he was unlike the others. All the other hardwood trees in the forest that surrounded him, were very different from him. They had leaves of all shapes and sizes. Their leaves even changed to bright colors in the Autumn.

He, on the other hand, had only evergreen needles. The other trees were made of hardwood, used for good quality lumber. However, he had only soft, brittle bark and soft wood. The maples, oaks, aspen, and sycamores that surrounded him would all change the colors of their leaves in October, and then drop them to the ground. And every October, he would swing his branches and hope for the wind to blow his way, but no matter how hard he tried, he never could do what the other trees did. He was stuck with his needles.

However, one Winter, the pine tree began to notice something new. He could see, just beyond the trees that were around him. Before this winter, he had never been tall enough to see. But with all of their leaves gone and with new growth, Pine could see just a bit beyond the hardwoods. And he thought he could see—other trees, across the creek—that looked like him?

Pine couldn't believe it—that there were other trees, besides him, that looked like him. That had needles, like him. That were green in the winter, like him. He wanted so badly to be on the other side of the creek and to be with the other trees that looked like him, but no matter how hard he tried to move, he was rooted in place.

And soon, Winter was over, Spring came, and the foliage of the hardwoods returned. The pine tree spent that year wishing to see across the creek, into the other forest, hoping to catch a glimpse of the other trees that looked like him.

Eventually, Autumn came, and he saw them again, and this year, he was taller. He could see them much better, much clearer. He saw their limbs, their trunks—even their needles. And they all look just like him. But he was stuck on this side of the creek.

One night during the Winter, when Pine was wishing to be with the trees that were like him, something happened.

Because it was Winter, all the trees around him had lost all of their leaves, which meant they couldn't provide any shelter to any of the animals and couldn't produce any fruit—not until the Spring. But Pine—he had his needles.

And on this night, a small chipmunk, lost and in need of shelter from the cold, came to Pine. His family too, was across the creek. But he couldn't cross it. And none of the hardwood trees were able to give him a home for the Winter.

So Pine obliged.

And Pine began to notice something again: there were other animals that lived in his branches every year during Winter, because they had nowhere else to go, and he was the only one who was still green.

He looked across the creek at the other trees like him and saw that those trees did the same thing.

It was because he was different and evergreen that he was good and served a purpose.

Pine began to imagine what he could do. And the taller he grew every year, the more he saw.

Every Winter, it was his time to shine.

Pine was stuck with his needles.

He was evergreen.

Pine was content with that.

Gem's Hidden Crystal

by: Ely Ganzer

In a land not too far away and a time not too long ago, a young man believed he had lost it all. Full of a sense of failure and overwhelmed by defeat, he was on a journey to find his way to something he did not know, or maybe it was a quest to escape everything that was haunting him.

On one cold and dreary morning he found himself walking down a trail he had never been before. As he turned onto this well-beaten path, a small, unnoticeable trail caught his eye as it led him through the mossy branch of a long-forgotten creek bed that was slightly overgrown with every kind of tree that bore every kind of thorns. As he made his way down the mossy branch, the trail had grown thicker and harder to pass to the point he was on his hands and knees, just trying to find his way out. While inching along, he stumbled upon a drive that opened up and led to a larger, old, forgotten house.

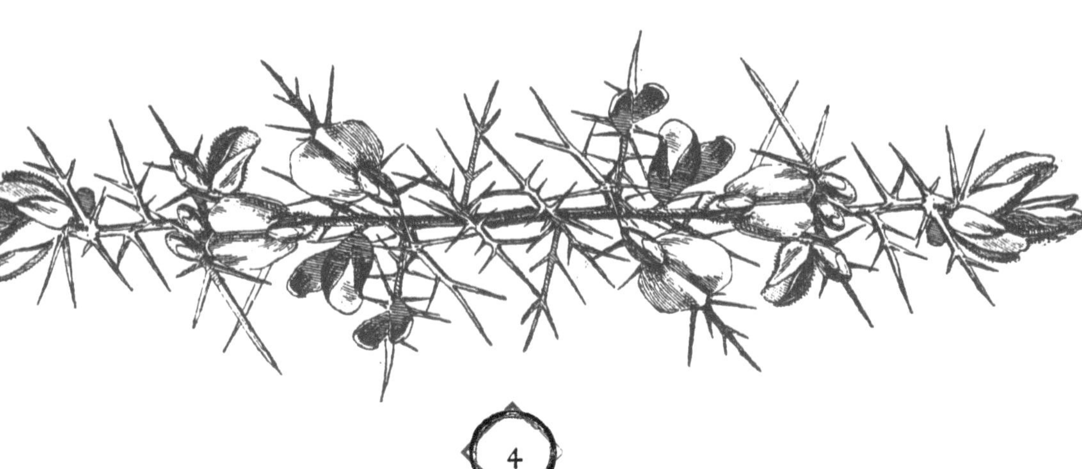

This old house was full of memories and mysteries the previous family had left behind. So the young man looked around at all that he saw, gathering his thoughts, believing that he had found the place he was looking for. Heading back down the mossy branch to go and gather the few things he hadn't lost, he had three treasures to bring to this old, forgotten house filled with memories and mysteries. One of the treasures sparkled and shined, this was the one he held closest to his heart. The second of these treasures lost a bit of their luster. He was confused and somewhat perplexed about this treasure because he didn't know how to handle it anymore, and the other which was at one time the grandest of them all, left him with a sense of uncertainty because he began to realize this treasure was not at all like he thought it should be.

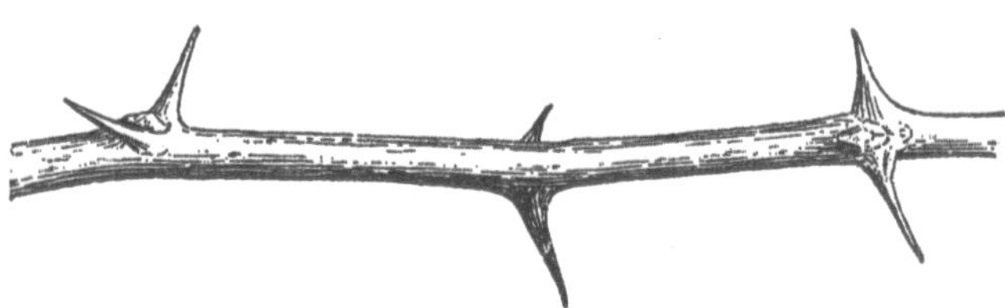

Days later, the young man returned with his three treasures: the one he kept close to his heart, the one he was confused and perplexed about, and the other that made him full of uncertainties. He placed the first two treasures in the house and went with the third to look through the woods that bore every kind of thorn to see what could be found. Returning to the old house full of mysteries and memories, it began to seem more like home.

So it was as time went on - days, weeks, months, maybe even a year, the first two treasures began to shine more and looked like what they indeed were. But those woods that bore every kind of thorn called to him, bidding him to come, or maybe it was the third treasure that called him out into those woods that bore every kind of thorn. He found himself in those woods, trying to find everything he thought he had lost day after day, month after month. As time went on, the old house that was once full of mystery and memories became filled with light and life as the first two treasures sparkled and showed all the splendor of a perfectly-cut gem that has the grace that reflects the brilliance of light. But those woods that bore every kind of thorn is where the young man spent a vast amount of his time, and as his understanding deepened and grew of the treasure that is the grandest of them all, those woods that bore every kind of thorn became alive and teeming with life that was budding forth as the light and life filled those woods and the old house, which now was home.

Others who were lost and full of a sense of failure and despair found themselves drawn to the light and life that shown forth down an old forgotten trail of the mossy branch which bore every kind of thorn. Because gems' hidden crystal shown with all the splendor of a perfectly cut gem that was full of the grace that reflects the brilliance of light and life.

A Crow's Rest

by: Joshua Robertson

Pining in a snows drift, swept deep and wide. A crow, keenly perched on a branch fastens his gaze across a glade covered white.
He spreads his wings with intent, frantically through the current, he fights. Faster and faster-still he beats them into the moonlit, silhouetted night.
He climbs just oe'r treetop, now beating softer with deliberate poise.
Letting vigor's air and passion's wind carry him aloft the glade
His eyes are of a special kind, unencumbered by stinging white. His body sleek, dark, yet shimmering bright.
Lonely are the thoughts of a bird so bare. Or perchance, it is I, the one who doth longingly stare.
Standing in a glade so vast, yet I, so small. How I long to soar in winter's storm, above the glade... above it all.

Fishie

A collection of short stories by: Isaac LaVigne

A vast array of coral reefs fills the ocean expanse-vibrant, jubilant, teeming with color and life. A manifold spread of diverse sea creatures drifts through the abyss. Sea turtles graze past grand schools of fish. Seahorses gallop and prance along to the next race. Jellyfish construct a trampoline park of misery. Starfish twinkle on the sands of time itself.

Among it all, a big-eyed, slender-bodied, peculiar-looking fish. Quiet. Observant. Contemplative. A lanternfish by the name of Fishie. Fishie. F-I-S-H-I-E. Fishie. A whimsical little creature. Fishie is quite different from all the other lanternfish. For starters, Fishie likes to swim on the surface during the day. All the other lanternfish spend their days in the darkest parts of the waters. But as the sun sets, they slowly trickle to the surface before nightfall. Unlike the others, Fishie prefers to explore the uncharted waters by night. Each time he sways to the bottom of the ocean, he passes different species of lanternfish. As each zonal species passes him on the way to the surface, he is ignored.
He seemingly doesn't mind.
He likes to swim alone anyways.

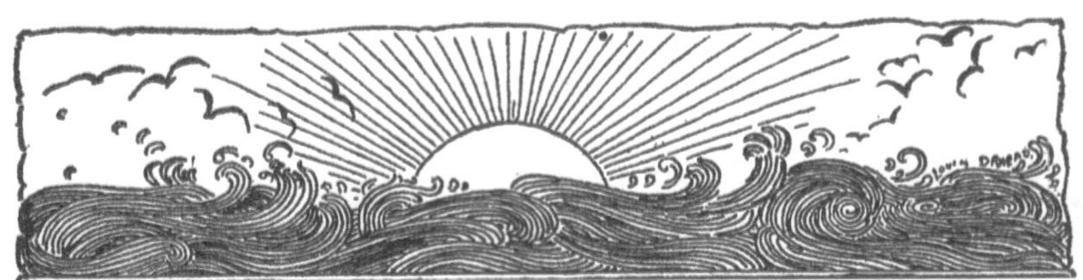

The further down he explored, the more he realized that a honey-yellow light, constant and gentle, glowed within him. The light is activated by the photophores hidden on the underside of his belly. The light, yes, dark in hue, yes, not as noticeable as the other lanternfish, is still a light. All differences aside, Fishie does know this... He loves carrying nutrients throughout the ocean. Nitrogen, Phosphorus, Silicon. Each of these elements is essential to the cycling of nutrients that allow the ocean ecosystem to flourish. Fishie knows that delivering these bubbles of hope across the ocean brings him joy, even if it means traveling to the deep, dark ocean floor.

Ultimately, Fishie knows who HE is. He is a messenger. He is bioluminescent. He is a lanternfish. And the waves shimmered in the warmth of the sun.

One day, Fishie saw something swirling in the golden-orange rays of the sun. It was a large school of bristlemouth fishes, mindlessly migrating. Fishie couldn't help but notice the light emanating from the school. It was translucent, almost ghostly. He joined them, hoping to be allowed to tag along. After some time, Fishie notices that his light didn't shine as brightly as the bristlemouth fish, let alone the lanternfish. Their dim, ethereal light collectively bathed the ocean in a semblance of warmth. Fishie, in contrast, was counter-illuminating. His scales shifting to camouflage seamlessly with the ambient light of the sea. No one saw him, no one noticed. And the waves shimmered in the warmth of the sun.

One day, time moved quickly. Fishie was eager, excited, elated. He had spent the majority of the day carrying little blue bubbles of Silicon all across the coral reef system. The task, though important, had begun to feel monotonous. Tonight, he would take Phosphorus to the ocean floor. He raced and he swayed and he raced and he swayed to the bottom of the ocean. Out of breath and gasping for air, he finally came across a rustic, decrepit marine crab. The crimson crab, eyeing him with impatience, blurted, 'What took so long?' Fishie was shocked and dismayed. He explained how he was new in carrying these essential elements to different parts of the ecosystem. He tells the crab how he's trying, how he wants to be faster, and how he hopes to successfully carry these elements throughout the ocean entirely. The crab interrupted him. "You're too small, too slow, too dull in light. You simply cannot." And he snatched the bubble and scurried back into the darkness of his lair. Dejected, Fishie stumbled back to the surface.

"Bring it to me." The voice, soft and gentle.

Fishie turned around to see a glowing plant—a phytoplankton. His light was warm and inviting. "Nitrogen, Phosphorus, Silicon. Bring it to me," the plant said. Fishie agreed.

And the waves shimmered in the warmth of the sun.

One day, Fishie was overwhelmed.

He had promised himself that once or twice a week, he would discover new territories around the coast. This would allow him to supply more habitats with necessary nutrients, but today, he felt like he was forgetting something. Suddenly, he remembered the Phytoplankton plant's request. He quickly collected the elements and ventured on his way, cautiously approaching the darkness yet again. The waters before him were cold and unyielding. The undercurrent ripping him across the deep trenches of the abyss.

Blackness surrounded him. The light under his belly flickered. He was lost. But in the distance, a fully-lit lantern glowed. It was Phytoplankton. Fishie rushed towards it, fearful that he would lose sight of the guiding light. As he approached the bioluminescent presence of the plant, frustration built inside him. Why did his light fail to make a path? Why was he the one tasked with descending back into the depths of darkness? Why couldn't someone else deliver these elements for once? What about this envoy agony did he find so much solace in? And how could he improve if he insisted on carrying these elements across the vast ocean? The plant patiently gestured toward Fishie's light. It was radiating. Fishie smiled.

"Thank you."

And the waves shimmered in the warmth of the sun.

One day, night fell upon the ecosystem, sweeping over it in an instant. All the various species of lanternfish resorted to the surface, where the coral reefs sparkled, reflecting the purplish light of the moon. Fishie, oblivious to the beauty cast by the moon, departed into the unknown blackness. After aimlessly swimming for some time, Fishie stumbled across a ghostly white light.

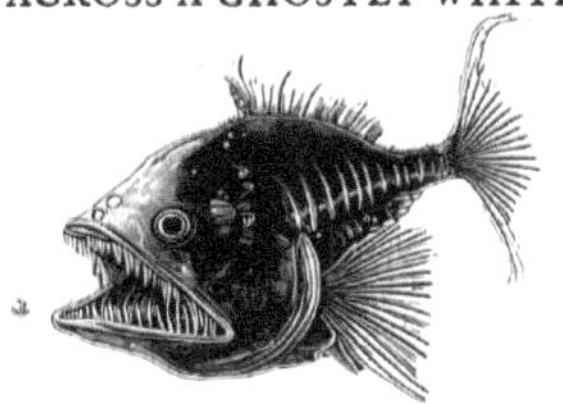

This was no ordinary light. It moved around rapidly, violently, spontaneously—emanating from a mysterious creature. It was an anglerfish. At first, he didn't notice her, fixated on the light dangling in front of him, a glowing lure extending from her dorsal fin. Fishie observed from afar, unsure of what to say. Perhaps a greeting? A question? Or maybe even a challenge? She turned toward him. "Who are you? How do you glow? Where do you come from? What are you doing here?" Fishie remained silent. She urged him to come closer. Reluctantly, but drawn by curiosity, Fishie swam toward her. She seemed alone—and perhaps desperate for connection. Maybe she needed help? He circled around her, inch by inch, his hesitation warring with his curiosity. The gravity of the moment tugged at his conscience. Restless, she screamed, "Say something!" Fishie wasn't startled though. He was completely encapsulated by her glow. Fishie floated closer, inch by inch, still unaware of the danger. Her jaw slowly closed around him, the pressure growing.

And the waves shimmered in the warmth of the sun.

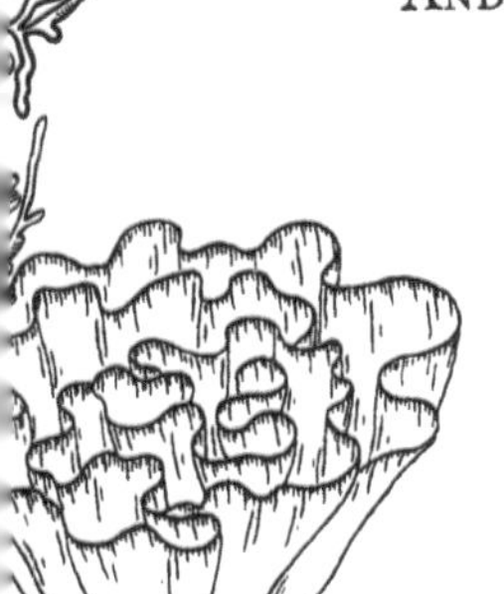

One day, a group of sharks floated near the surface of the warm waters. Distanced, yet piqued, Fishie observed from the coast. They were massive—several meters long, stocky, robust, and stoic. At first, Fishie might have felt apprehensive, but today he felt unusually calm. He cautiously approached them.

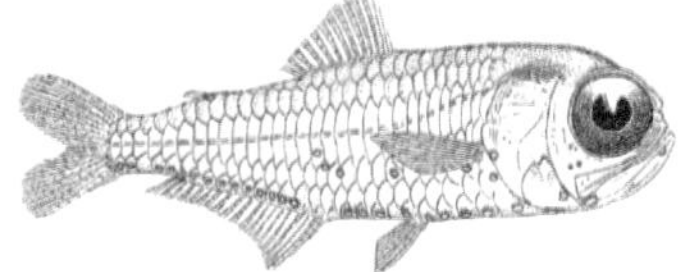

One by one, the sharks turned towards him, their movements slow and easy. Through a quick conversation, Fishie learned that they weren't from the coast like him. They traveled across different regions of the ocean, delivering stories—stories filled with hope and joy. The ocean was dark enough, they explained, and needed light. Something about them made Fishie feel as if he knew them. Fishie, in turn, shared his love for carrying the little nutrient bubbles across the sea. He paused, as though unsure how to ask for help. The sharks, sensing his hesitation, looked at him kindly. "Do you need help?" one of them asked. Fishie nodded, "Yes." He explained how to carry the bubbles, and the sharks learned quickly. Although they couldn't stay long, they helped him as much as they could. Fishie felt the weight of his task lighten. Before they left, one of the sharks turned to him and said, "Your size may deceive, but your light shines brightly."

And the waves shimmered in the warmth of the sun.

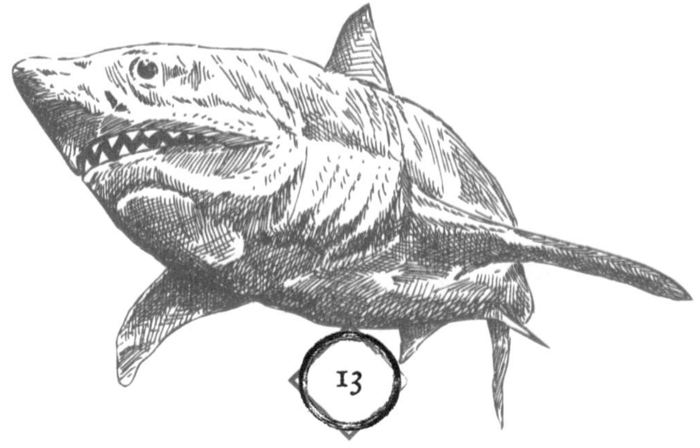

One day, after many years had passed, Fishie was older, wiser, and more experienced. He had traveled far and endured much—battered, tired, yet still inspired. As he began his descent into the depths of the ocean once again, a place he knew all too well, his light paved the way.

The deep blue sea welcomed him, his unique glow casting patterns on his smooth scales, cutting through the calm and raging waves of the vast ocean. The waves shimmer, a dance of light in the sun's embrace.

The Battle Within

By: Pedro Suazolaboy

Once upon a time, Henry, a soldier forged by the fires of World War II, returned home to a life he could barely recognize. After years of surviving battlefields where discipline and control meant life or death, he now faced something far more unfamiliar: a home filled with love, tenderness, and expectation. Awaiting him was his wife, Claire, whose unwavering letters had been his anchor during the war, and their newborn son, Samuel—a child he had only learned of after the fighting had ended.

At first, Henry stood at a distance, unable to connect with this new reality. His wife's soft words and their child's tiny cries felt foreign, even unnerving. Samuel, fragile and needy, reminded Henry of a part of himself he had spent years trying to forget. The truth was, Henry had no blueprint for fatherhood. His own father had left when he was young, leaving him to grow up under the weight of scarcity and silence. Now, he was expected to provide the love and guidance he had never received.

Frustration grew with each passing day. When Samuel cried inconsolably at night, Henry would pace, his hands shaking with helplessness, his mind yearning for the order and predictability of a soldier's life. Claire, patient but weary, tried to guide him, but Henry often met her words with irritation. "You don't understand," he'd say, withdrawing. He found himself treating his home like a command post, barking orders when Samuel wouldn't stop crying or when Claire didn't respond as quickly as a soldier would. His family, however, didn't respond to commands.

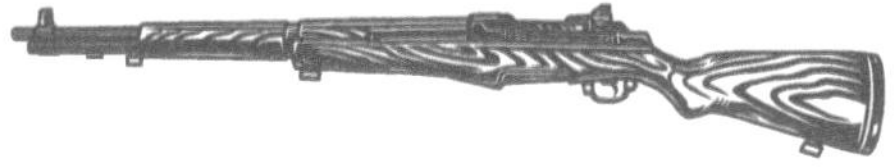

They needed love, gentleness, and understanding... qualities he had buried deep under the weight of war.

The cracks in their relationship began to show. Arguments became more frequent, usually ending with Henry walking away, retreating into himself rather than engaging with the messiness of emotions. Claire pleaded with him, not for perfection, but for presence. "You're here, Henry, but you're not here," she said one night after he had brushed off her concerns. Her words hit him like shrapnel, but still, he didn't know how to respond.

One night, after a heated argument, Henry stormed out into the cold. Samuel's cries still echoed in his ears, and Claire's tearful voice clung to him like a shadow. He needed to escape. He began running, the cool night air biting at his face, his mind racing with anger, shame, and confusion. Claire, desperate to reach him, ran after him, calling his name throughout the neighborhood. When she caught up, she grabbed his arm and shoved him, tears streaming down her face. "Don't you see what you're doing to us? To me?" she cried. For a moment, Henry froze. The look in her eyes—raw, pleading, broken—left him paralyzed. He realized then how much she was hurting, how his silence and distance had wounded her more deeply than his words ever could.

But still, his shame pushed him away. He let her walk back to the house alone, believing that distance would bring clarity to his dilemma. He kept running, convincing himself that exhaustion might quiet the storm inside him.

When Henry returned hours later, he found Claire kneeling in the small garden behind their home. Her dress was torn, dirt clung to her hands, and she was planting seeds in the moonlight with trembling fingers. She was surrounded by the same flowers she had lovingly tended for years—roses, daisies, and vegetables sprouting in neat rows. In her distress, she had turned to the soil, pouring her emotions into the act of nurturing life. It was her way of grounding herself, of making sense of pain... through creation.

Henry approached hesitantly, unsure of what to say. Claire didn't look at him but continued pressing seeds into the earth. Finally, she spoke, her voice raw but steady. "Do you know why I garden, Henry? Because it reminds me that everything worth having takes time, care, and patience. You plant a seed, and it feels like nothing's happening. But if you pour into it, if you tend to it, one day, it grows. It becomes something beautiful, something alive. That's what I've been trying to teach you—about Samuel, about us."

Her words struck a chord deep within Henry. For the first time, he saw his wife's garden not as a hobby, but as a reflection of her soul—a place where she channeled her emotions, her hope, and her love. He realized that, like the garden, his family needed tending, not control. They needed his presence, his care, his willingness to stay and nurture, even when the process felt slow and uncertain.

Henry knelt beside her, his hands shivering as he reached for the soil. "Teach me," he said quietly. "Teach me how to do this."

Claire finally turned to him, her tear-streaked face softening. She placed a seed in his hand, pressing his fingers around it. Together, they buried it in the earth, a quiet symbol of renewal.

In that moment,
Henry understood that being a father and husband wasn't about
control; it was about surrendering to the
chaos of love, about showing up even
when you don't have all the answers.

That night marked the beginning of
Henry's journey—not just as a
father or husband, but as a man
learning to nurture and grow
alongside his family.

Acceptance's Call

By: Joshua Robertson

There was once a boy who felt unseen. He lived in a small, ordinary house at the edge of a great and bright and humming world. The boy learned to navigate his family, knowing their opinions of him from an early age. His father was a man of great wisdom, but he spent his days staring beyond the boy, as though searching for something just out of reach. His gaze never resting. To the boy, his father's wisdom and affection felt like a distant star—beautiful, but cold.

His mother, though no less present, was sharp in her affections towards the boy, her regret palpable.. Her heart belonged to only her first-born, "her pride." The boy... rejected. The eldest was strong and clever, and an inherent reflection of his mother and father, in ways. He won the praise of friends and the love of his parents, while the boy stood in the shadow of his favor. "I wish you were more like him," his mother would say when the boy stumbled. "You will learn in time," his father would murmur absently.

And so the boy grew up — existing like a name spoken in an empty room. One day, when the days of isolation and being ignored grew too many, the boy could endure no more. "If I do not belong here," he said to himself, "then I will seek my place elsewhere."
He packed what little he owned, and set off down the road into the great and bright and humming world beyond.

When the boy arrived at the edge of the forest, his future of independence stretching before him, he briefly hesitated. Fear was slipping its noose around him, when suddenly... it all fell silent. He heard a still small voice. One that sounded familiar during his time in a house so big and a life so alone. It had been comfort during the darkest night. This time it offered courage: "There is a journey for you, boy. Follow truth's path."

His journeying here turned into years, familiarizing himself to the forest he now called home. The still small voice who met him at the forest's entrance sweetly guiding him forward.

As he continued on, the boy walked through a shaded part of the forest, where the trees grew close and their branches wove a dense canopy overhead. It was there he met Miragen, sitting by a calming stream, her hands busy weaving a garland of wildflowers. She looked up at him with a smile that seemed to warm the air. "Oh, you poor thing," she said, standing and brushing off her skirt. "You look so tired, so worn." She came close, with outstretched hands. Her eyes sharp and unreadable. "I am," the boy admitted. "The road is long, and I am unsure of where it leads."

"Come," said Miragen, draping a soft and heavy cloak over his shoulders. "There is no reason to haste. Rest here and I will keep you safe. You need not worry about the road ahead. Let me look after you."

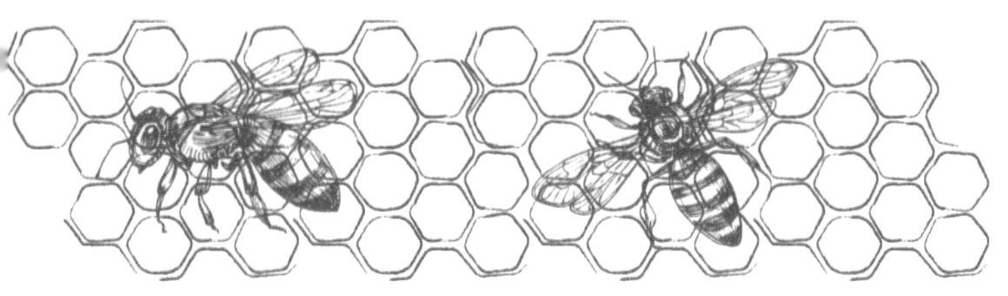

Her voice was so soothing, her presence so comforting, that the boy sank down by the stream. Miragen hummed a lullaby, her hands ever weaving, and the boy felt a rare peace.

But as the boy awoke and the yellow sky bled into an amber hue, the cloak grew heavier. He found it harder to move, harder still to think.

"Miragen," he said, his voice weak and gasps heavy. "I think I must continue." "Why?" she asked, tilting her head. "The world is cruel and harsh. Stay here where it is safe." Her smile remained, but her hands tightened the cloak around him. The boy struggled to his feet, the weight of the cloak almost unbearable. Unexpextedly, the still, small voice cut sharply through the panic and emboldened him. "Your care feels like chains," he said. "What has been rest, is now restraint"!

His resentment of the manipulation vitalized his hand.

He tore off the yoke, the cloak falling with him to his knees. Miragen stayed silent. Maddened, the young boy rose to his feet, lifted his gaze, and regained the path. Miragen watched him go, still smiling, but her eyes glittered like the edge of a blade.

"Keep moving", the still small voice urged. The boy agreeably moved on.

He reflected on the peace nearly attained, the care closely felt. He resented the lies concealed in honey. Yet, he ached for the sereneity of such an approval.

For a moment he was chosen. For a moment...

The boy grew in both years and wisdom, time allowing him to bud into the expression of a young man. But the forest was not home. And so, with the small still voice guiding him gently forward, he continued his journey. The forest relented to open fields where the grass rippled like the ocean under the wind. His journeying here turned into years, familiarizing himself to the fileds he now called home.

One day, quickened feet upon the path caught his attention. There, he encountered Aspiro, a man with a sharp grin and a confident stride. His clothes were splendid, though frayed at the edges, and his hands gestured grandly as he spoke. "Ah, a traveler!" Aspiro exclaimed. "Surely you seek greatness? Adventure? Glory?"

"I seek my place," the young man replied.

"...and wisdom should it be found."

"Then you mustn't dawdle!" Aspiro declared. "Look around you. If you strive, this great and bright and humming world will marvel at you. The mountaintop awaits, the horizon calls! There is no time to waste." His eloquence and persuasion like that of a songbird, and the young man felt a spark of excitement.

He quickened his pace, spurred on by Aspiro's urging.

However, the faster they walked, the less the young man could enjoy the world around him. The flowers blurred past; the song of the birds faded under the rush of wind.

"Slow down," he said. "I cannot keep this pace."
"Slow down?" Aspiro laughed, incredulous. "The world is not for the sluggish. Only those who strive will achieve greatness. Look at me – Throughout my journey I have always pushed forward, always reached higher, and there is still more to achieve."

The young man looked anew at Aspiro's worn shoes, the frayed hems of his once-fine clothes. He realized that, for all his confidence, Aspiro had never truly rested, never truly arrived, never truly belonged.
Again, a still small voice from within heartened him to speak out.
"You chase what you cannot catch," the young man said softly. "As do I, perhaps. But, your wisdom leaves no room for joy, and never have you belonged."

Immediately the still small voice urged, "Keep moving."
The young man agreeably moved on.
Aspiro scoffed but did not follow as he turned and walked away. As the young man regained the path, his pace was slower, more measured. The reverberations of achievement and recognition filled his mind and fluttered his heart.
Yet, he knew that chasing wind would leave him with empty sails.
For a moment he was chosen. For a moment...

Years began to slip by, and the young man grew. His countenance became that of a venerable and wiser man. But the field was not home. And so, with the small still voice guiding him gently forward, he continued his journey.

In a rocky gorge, where the path was steep and the air felt heavy, the wiser man hewed a life in canyon and ridges. His journeying here turned into years, familiarizing himself to the gorge he now called home. One day, a distant vibration stirred the earth. It was here the wiser man met Feraxus. He was a towering figure with a scarred face and smoldering eyes. His fists were clenched, and his voice rumbled like distant thunder.

"Why do you hesitate?" Feraxus demanded as the wiser man approached. "The world is harsh. If you do not seize what is yours, or what should be, it will crush you. If you do not fiercely stand, you will idlely fall!" The wiser man stopped, the uncertainty threatening. "I do not wish to crush anyone."

"Then you are weak!" Feraxus bellowed, his voice reverberating the cavity of his chest. "You must arrest strength, you must satiate appetite. Strength is power! Appetite, your bliss! You want wisdom? I will teach you this: Fight for what you want, or it will be taken from you. Pursue your hungers or you will find yourself empty and abandoned."

His words lit a fire in the man's chest. He clenched his fists, stood taller, and shouted into the gorge. The echoes filled him with a fleeting sense of power. Passion welled within him!

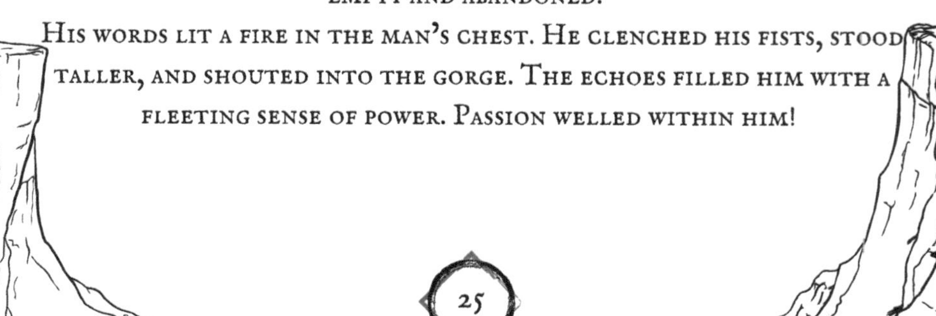

But as he turned to face the path ahead, he realized he was alone. Feraxus stood apart, his fists still raised, but there was no one at his side either. His cravings fulfilled had still left him unsatiated, isolated... abandoned.

"Is this all power and passion gives?" the wiser man asked. "To be feared, to be alone?"
Feraxus snarled, his voice low. "Better alone than weak."
The wiser man shook his head. Again, the familiar voice gave uttereance from within once more: "Your wisdom burns too hot." He repulsed. "It scorches everything it touches!"

"Keep moving", the still small voice urged.
The wiser man agreeably moved on, leaving Feraxus to his lonely vigil. The wiser man saw unveiled the detestation and dread of hoarding power and chasing bliss. "Perhaps," he thought, "passion and power could be exercised for the good of others. Perhaps..."
For a moment he was chosen. For a moment...

Finally, after many years of journeying, the wiser man came to a quiet glade. A brook wound through the grass, and beside it sat Selvyn, a small figure with gentle eyes. Her hands were folded in her lap, and her smile was soft and unassuming.

"You look weary," she said as the older man approached. Unsure, yet curious, he tried to place the familiar voice, soothing as pure honey.

"I am," he replied, moving closer to the unassuming figure.

Selvyn offered him a place to sit and a cup of cool spring water. She did not speak for awhile, letting him drink, and recover, and truly rest.

"Why do you travel?" she asked eventually.

"I seek a place to belong, and I seek wisdom should it be found," the older man replied.

"And what have you found?"

The older man hesitated. "I have met those who cared too much, those who raced too fast, and those who burned too brightly. Their wisdom seemed strong, but it left me heavy, breathless, and alone."

Selvyn nodded. "True wisdom is truthful," she said. "It does not bind, or race, or burn. It waits. It listens. It gives unreservedly."

One day, during his reflective walks, the esteemed boy's path led him to the edge of a ravine. Then he heard it...

The still small familiar voice "Keep moving" it urged, "your journey is leading where you are needed most."

The road was narrow, the wind howling as if to warn of the danger below. On the other side, he saw a child—no older than seven—clinging to a crumbling ledge. Below was the revelation of his attempted escape, a dark and seething creature of the night, hungry and ravenous. The child's cries for help barely carried over the wind.

The boy's heart pounded. The distance to the other side was vast, the ground beneath him loose and treacherous. Saving the child would mean risking his own life.

He hesitated, fear creeping into his veins like ice. Suddenly, he heard the voices of his journey —those he had met long ago.

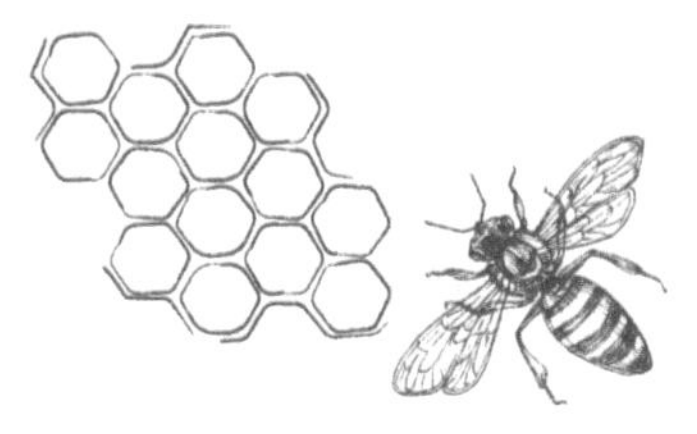

"Stay where you are," Miragen cooed, her voice carried by the wind. "You've already endured so much. Let the world take care of itself; it always does. You are safe here. The child will find his way—children are resilient. Stay safe, for now you are chosen."

The boy looked down at the solid ground beneath his feet, the temptation of safety pulling at him like a warm cloak. But in his heart, he knew the child would not survive the darkness below.

"Run!" Aspiro shouted, his words bursting with urgency. "Leap across the gap! Show the world what you're made of. Heroes don't hesitate—they act! This is your moment! Claim greatness! Earn your title"

The boy's pulse quickened. He stepped back, ready to sprint, ready to attack, but doubt took hold. What if he failed? What if his eagerness caused them both to perish? Aspiro's fervor felt reckless.

"Do not waste time," Feraxus growled, his tone sharp and commanding. "Claw your way to him, no matter the cost! If you want to save him, you must crush your fear, and crush any who stand in your way! Or... decide to leave now... You have what you've always desired. Why would you waste it all for this... BOY. Take the path away so you may hold tightly to what you desire."

The boy clenched his fists, anger and passion surging through him. But then he remembered Feraxus's isolation, the loneliness that came with his unyielding strength and pursuit of harmful, selfish desire. Would he save the child, only to lose himself in the process? In his heart, he knew he could not abandon this innocence in need of rescue.

Finally, the boy heard the voice that had guided him his whole life - Selvyn, her voice calm and steady. "Step forward boy. Not because you are fearless, but because it is right. You may not succeed, but the endeavor alone is the mark of a life well-lived."

The boy's chest tightened, not with fear, but with clarity. Selvyn's words carried no promises of glory or safety or desire. But in his heart, he knew they carried the truth.

He dropped his satchel and took the first step forward. Each movement was deliberate, each step mindful of the unsettled stones beneath his feet and the darkeness pacing below. The ravine yawned below him, but he focused on the child's eyes, wide with desperation.

"Hold on!" the boy called. "I'm coming!"

He reached the edge of the ledge and stretched his hand across the gap. The child's fingers were small and cold, barely gripping his own. As the ground beneath the child gave way, the boy braced himself, pulling with all his might.

But the edge crumbled.

The boy, older and more frail in might, mustered all the strength that he could and threw himself downward, using his own weight and momentum to pull the child to safety. For a brief moment, their eyes met—a silent understanding passing between them.

He fell, the wind rushing past him in a deafening roar. As the ground rose to meet him, the dark and seething creature of the night waiting to devour, his thoughts were not of fear, but of a chosen and worthy life. In that moment, he realized he had become more than a forgotten second son. He had become a thread in the tapestry of life, woven by genuine care, wise discernment, bridled strength, and pure kindness. He had been chosen—not by his family, not by the world, but by something greater. This act gave utterance of it.

For the last time, the boy closed his eyes.

The child stood trembling at the edge of the ravine, tears streaming down his face.

Selvyn appeared beside him, placing a gentle hand on his shoulder.

"Your life was spared," she said softly.

The child, shocked and yet unphased by her presence asked, "Why... why did he do this for me? He was a beacon of light for us all!"

Selvyn allowed the child to contemplate the sacrifice. "Remember the boy's courage." She insisted. "Carry it with you, not as a burden, but as a light. There is a journey before you, boy."

Miragen, Aspiro, and Feraxus lingered in the shadows, silent and contemplative. Their wisdom, too, had played its part, though they seemed humbled by the final act of the boy.

The child, walked somberly away from the ravine, Selvyn lingering by his side. His steps were hesitant but steady. Though he did not know it, he carried the boy's legacy in his heart—a legacy of flawed yet profound wisdom, of sacrifice, and of the quiet strength that kindness brings. Selvyn turned to the child. "To listen for quiet wisdom is to hear the truth. To be rejected is not to be without purpose. And to give oneself for another is a call of all those who are chosen." Bereaved, yet comforted the child walked on to the edge of a great and bright and humming world.

The villagers built a small cairn of stones by the river. And in the years to come, those who passed by would pause and say:
"Here lies one who chose, though was not chosen."

In The Shadow of Valleys

By: Jonny Gallegos
Adopted By: Joshua Robertson

Once there was a man who lived in a village known by its valley. From the stories and legends that had stretched far and wide, there was no other valley like his. None that grew the same crops, or held the same customs, or sang the same songs. The valleys were separated. Vanity grew their peaks tall, and the shadows over their valley, long.

Day after day, the man watched the sun rise and set by its light shining upon the crest of each side of their valley. The sun stayed overhead for a brief moment in time before hiding itself away again. What was grown in their valley was made by the soft indirect light that echoed the warmth of the sun.

One day, the man decided that the resentment and discontent for his valley had reached its peak. His curiosity grew and he knew he wanted to try to move on. Despite the warnings and encouragement towards contentment from others, the man was determined. He packed up only a few belongings, for he did not want the extra weight of a past life with him as he went. He also decided to take some seed from the special harvests of his village's fields. He resolved that wherever he should go next, he might be able to take with him the unique and enriching nourishment of his village.

The man began his ascent up the steep embankment of rock and stone. This was his first attempt at such an escape. He climbed the shadowed cliff side. His hands became torn from the edges, his face weathered by the wind. With sacrifice, difficulty, and loss, he climbed.

Eventually, he reached the summit

A sense of awe overcame him as he stood atop the peak.
The sun was the grandest thing he had ever seen. It was resplendent, large and powerful. Never had he seen it with such unencumbered wonder.
Behind him, in a shrouded valley was the familiarity of a previous life. Ahead, he could vaguely make out a new valley, a new village, a new life.

The man began his decent. Carefully he made his way to the village center. The shock on the villagers' faces gave semblance to the rare and utter magnitude of his arrival. He was heralded in his new village. Adoration for the seeds he provided that they had never seen. Intrigue for his customs that were new, for the songs that had never been sung in their valley. Here the man felt home

Days came and went. Months and even years...
One day, the man decided that the resentment and discontent for his valley had reached its peak. His curiosity grew, and he knew he wanted to try to move on. Despite the warnings and encouragement towards contentment from others, the man was determined. He packed up only a few belongings, for he did not want the extra weight of a past life with him as he went. He also decided to take some seed from the special harvests of his new village's fields, as well as the village from his beginning valley.

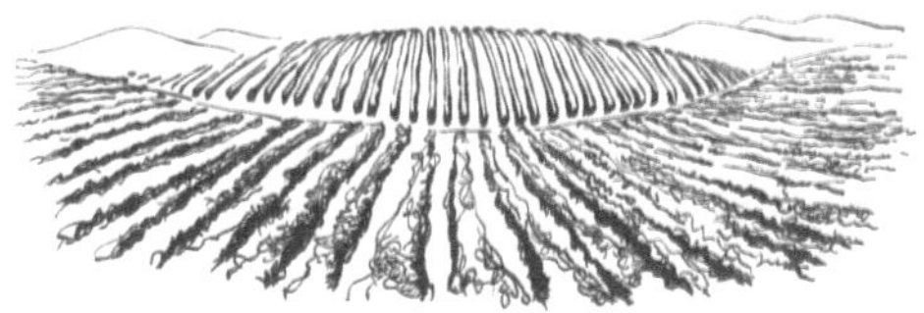

He climbed the shadowed cliff side. His hands became torn from the edges, his face weathered by the wind. With sacrifice, with difficulty, with loss, he climbed.

Eventually, he reached the summit.

Once again he stood in awe of the unbridled sun. Behind, a familiar life. Ahead, life anew.
He climbed down into this new valley and was once again was greeted by such an assembly. They marveled and extolled his culture, song, and seed. Here, the man felt at home.

Days came and went. Months and even years...
One day, the man decided...
He realized he was deciding the same thing once again. Here was another valley, slightly different from his beginning, slightly different than the next. Would it be any different than the next? Not in how it looks, its culture, its song, or its seed. But, to him. Would he... Could he find solace?

He climbed the shadowed cliff side. His hands were harder than the rock's edges, his face was weathered and unbothered by the wind. With sacrifice, with difficulty, with loss, he climbed.

Eventually, he reached the summit.

Behind him...
Stories, culture, song, and seed.
Before him...
"Contentment", he hoped... "Another valley", he was certain.

JoAnn's Finest

By: Jakob Dumke

A king of immeasurable wealth and power once lived in a castle in a greater kingdom on the southern edge of the continent, jutting out into the sea. The castle sat atop a hill, was surrounded by a moat, and was situated inside a greater kingdom. The southernmost part of the moat formed the southern border of the kingdom, it culminated in a waterfall that plunged into the great sea. The greater part of the kingdom was surrounded by an unbreachable wall with few entrances.

The king was born and raised in the castle. Reign was passed down to him at an early age after the people concluded that his parents would never return from their voyage. He was complacent in his rule. Thus, the people he led were complacent; they were not declining, nor were they thriving. The king would spend his days enjoying his wealth and admiring the intricate architecture of the castle from the inside. On occasion, he would venture out into the courtyard, but he ultimately refrained from leaving the castle grounds. As the young king grew older, his health began to decline. It was not enough to alarm him or anyone else. His days grew long with fatigue and weariness. The king would even find himself coughing up blood on occasion. Despite this, he ignored his affliction and pressed onward as if nothing was wrong.

One day, the king retired to his quarters after a long day of engaging in his kingly indulgences. He dressed himself for bed and laid himself down to rest. In an instant, he fell asleep.

The king sprang up from his bed in the middle of a noiseless night, drenched in a cold sweat. His heart was racing as he frantically scanned the room. He didn't take notice of anything save for a particularly dark corner of the room. Upon second inspection, the king saw Death sitting expectantly in the corner.

Eternity seemed to pass in silence as the king locked eyes with eyeless Death. After a long time, Death finally rose from the corner chair and walked to the king's bedside. The king sunk into his sheets, overcome by the weight of the presence of Death. Another long moment passed, when Death broke the silence and said to the king: "I am stripping you of your power. Now go to sleep".

Death passed his bony hand over the king's eyes, and he went to sleep.

It was afternoon the next day when the man was stirred by a ruckus at the door. He had slept in... The commotion intensified, and it wasn't long before the door gave way. Loyal subjects poured into the room. The ringleader cried out "King! King! Where are you, our king!?"

The man rose from his bed and replied, "Here I am."

The subjects gazed at each other in confusion. The ringleader quickly accused, "You are not our king... What have you done with our king? What have you done with our king!?"

In an instant, the subjects rallied and seized the man. They tore him from his room and dragged him out of the castle. Kicking and screaming, the man fought for his life to remain in his castle. He tarried and clawed, attempting to sink his fingers into anything that would anchor him to his home. Streaks of blood stained the beautiful walls and floor of the castle where the tips of the man's fingers were claimed. His fight was in vain, for he was eventually thrown out of the castle and handed over to the guards. Ceasing to be conscious from the arduous fight, the guards carried him out of the kingdom and left him outside of the front gate.

The man stirred from his unconsciousness. With little thought or consideration, he ran to the gate and began knocking. "Let me in! Let me in!" he cried, but there was never a reply. Yet, he persisted until he depleted himself of energy and fell unconscious again.

The man developed a new routine. His aim never changed his efforts only increased in intensity. Days and nights would pass. The man's rage intensified. He thrashed his body against the gate. He threw himself into the gate, clawed at the gate seeking entry, cried out until his tears dried up, and released what eventually became unintelligible, blood-curdling screams. He continued until he fell unconscious, and he would begin again as soon as he was able to rise. He pressed onward for days, weeks, months. He grew to no longer obey the sun as it rose and fell; he disregarded the natural order of things, instantiating his own rhythm for the world.

Evening time was approaching as the sun painted the landscape in warm amber when it began to rain. The man rose from the dirt he nested on as the rain kissed his skin. The rain soothed the rage and anger that had woven itself into the man's skin. For the first time since his arrival, he chose not to charge at the door; he woke, paused, and took a deep breath as the rain shyly washed over him. He looked down at himself and saw his body battered and bruised. He had grown thin; his ribs were showing from malnourishment. The man looked over to his right to see a small puddle forming. He walked over and looked deeply into the shallow puddle. He was cadaverous and unrecognizable. Looking up at the gate from a short distance, he saw the large bloody imprint on the gate from his endeavor at entry.

For the first time since the man was exiled, he turned around to look behind him; he turned away from the gate. A dirt road led down to a farm nestled in a wide valley. A log cabin was situated at the front of the farm. The farm had it all: grape vineyards, apple trees, fields of wheat, sheep, goats, pigs, cows, and even beehives. The man turned back to the gate, already the bloody imprint painted by his body began to haunt him. He exchanged glances to the farm and the gate, contemplating his past and possible future. Hesitantly, he departed and limped towards the cabin.

The sun quickly set into the horizon and the rain began to pour when the man crawled up the steps onto the wooden, lantern lit porch. He gathered himself up against the door. Engraved above the head of the door read: "JoAnn's". The man knocked. Immediately, a little old woman answered the door. "I have been expecting you" she said. "I have some dinner ready for you. Why don't you come in and join me". The man entered and sat at the table where dinner was already waiting for him.

JoAnn joined him at the table and continued eating.
The man hesitantly ate his food, as if he was testing each bite to discern if it was poisoned. He refused to look down at his food, scanning the room for potential danger. His behavior was that of a beast waiting to be ensnared.
"I have been looking forward to meeting you. I was wondering how long you were going to try your hand at that gate." The man did not reply. JoAnn spoke again, "I have prepared a cot for you to sleep on and have set aside a change of clothes for you. They were my Grandson's, I expect they will fit you well." JoAnn finished her dinner and went off to bed. The man remained at the table for some time, finishing his food. The food reinvigorated the man enough for him to carry himself to his cot, change his clothes, and fall asleep.

The sun was gently peering through the windows nearing the edge of the man's cot when the smell of breakfast was in the air. JoAnn was cooking, and it smelt good. "Breakfast is ready!" JoAnn calls out. The man rose from his cot and sat at the table. "I am happy you are here. I have been needing an extra set of hands." The man refused to answer. JoAnn finished her breakfast and left for her room. After her brief absence she emerged from her room in her work attire. JoAnn, a sweet old woman in her gardening gear said "well, we better get going! There is much work to be done."

She set forth, and the man followed from some distance behind her as she tended to the inhabitants of her land. The man refused to help all day, and JoAnn didn't ask him to. He carefully observed her from afar in silence as she harvested and watered the crops, worked the land, and fed the animals. They took time to sit and eat the lunch which JoAnn packed for them. After their brief recess, she faithfully continued working the land. That day, JoAnn had even butchered a cow all by herself.

The man glared resentfully towards the gate as he saw the cartman effortlessly enter the kingdom. Rage began to creep over him when he heard JoAnn call, "Dinner is ready!" He snapped out of his trance and returned inside for dinner.

This was their routine for some time. JoAnn would make breakfast, she would go out to work, the man would follow her and refuse to help or speak, they would have lunch together, finish the day's work, give goods to the cartman, have dinner, and go to sleep. Over time and many good meals, the man began to reinvigorate. His bruises and wounds healed, and his body slowly filled out with healthy weight.
One morning, as JoAnn and the man shared breakfast together, he looked up at her and shyly said, "Thank you for breakfast."

"Oh, so you do talk?" She chuckled in reply. Soon the cabin was filled with both of their laughter. On this day, as they set out to tend to the land and its inhabitants, the man began to help JoAnn. He took it upon himself to aid her in the work and to see the care of the land to completion. They grew closer together over time. As the days passed, the man would eventually find himself doing all the work joyfully while JoAnn sat and watched.

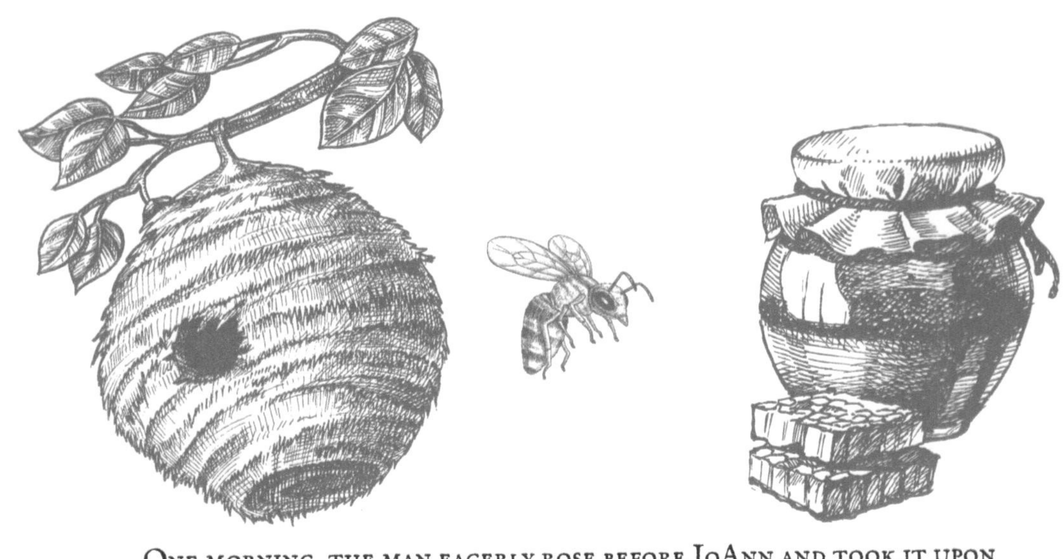

One morning, the man eagerly rose before JoAnn and took it upon himself to make breakfast for them.

Rising from her slumber, she was delighted by the surprise. Sharing breakfast together, JoAnn said, "I forgot to save a portion of the honey from the last harvest, and I am unsure if we will have enough to harvest today. It is unfortunate, I would really like some honey on my toast tomorrow morning. I am going to send you into the town to buy some for us."

Eager to care for JoAnn, the man accepts the task.

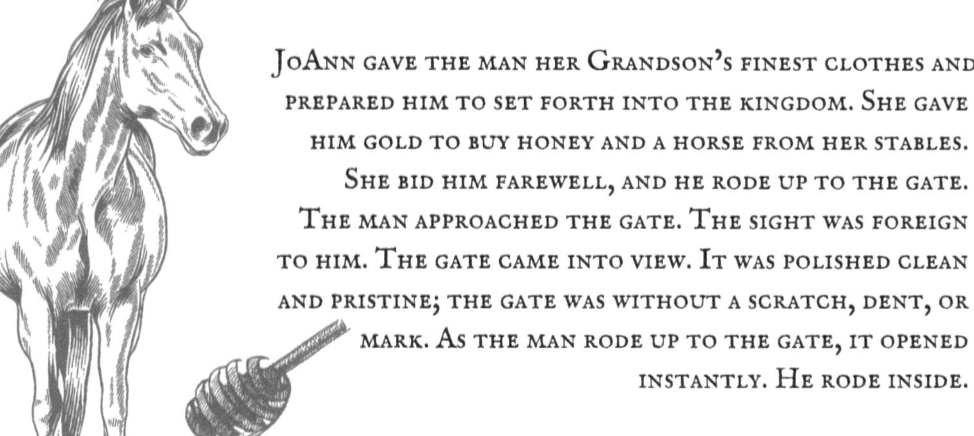

JoAnn gave the man her Grandson's finest clothes and prepared him to set forth into the kingdom. She gave him gold to buy honey and a horse from her stables. She bid him farewell, and he rode up to the gate. The man approached the gate. The sight was foreign to him. The gate came into view. It was polished clean and pristine; the gate was without a scratch, dent, or mark. As the man rode up to the gate, it opened instantly. He rode inside.

The quest for honey began. The horse hooves trotting on the stone road resounded through the lively kingdom when it dawned on the man, "I... I used to be king here. This used to be my kingdom." he thought. "This used to be my home. I wonder what became of my castle; I wonder if it still stands. Maybe I should go check. Surely, JoAnn would not mind this little side quest." The man pressed onward through the town and towards his former home.

Upon arrival, the castle was nowhere to be seen. He rode up to the mote that surrounded the castle and saw a great stone bridge over the water. He crossed the bridge and dismounted his horse to see the ruins of the castle and a great garden full of the most beautiful flowers in the land where it once stood. Many were in the garden, enjoying the flowers.

The man questioned a bystander, "What... What happened to the castle that once stood here?"

The bystander replied, "Our king... Our king had died, and there was no one to take his place. The people saw little use for the castle without a king to reside in it. We deconstructed it and used the pieces to build that great stone bridge." Perplexed, the man questioned, "I see... Without a king, who now do you serve?"

"After some time of wondering, we opened our hearts; the sun began to speak to us and lead us. Now, we take divine orders from the sun and thrive under its rule.", the bystander affirmed.

The man was fascinated by the response. He thanked the bystander for the information and for his time. He mounted his horse and went back into the town.

The man reached the market, tied up his horse, and dismounted. He entered the market in search of honey. As he began his investigation, he began to notice something.

All the vendors... On every sign in the market a brand could be seen: "JoAnn's Finest", it read. The man looked around the market amazed to see everyone in the market enjoying JoAnn's Finest goods. Jellies: meats,cheeses, illustrious wines, and bread.

Everywhere he looked he saw "JoAnn's Finest". He saw people enjoying JoAnn's Finest steaks, smearing JoAnn's Finest butter on JoAnn's Finest toast, drinking JoAnn's Finest wine, and even people putting JoAnn's Finest Honey in JoAnn's Finest coffee.

Honey! The reason for his quest. He asked the grey-bearded man drinking the coffee where the honey could be found, and he was pointed in the right direction. Approaching the vendor, the man reached into his pouch to pay for the honey. He had the exact amount of gold that he needed for one jar. He thanked the vendor for the honey and packed up to lave the market. Mounting his horse, he rode out of the kingdom.

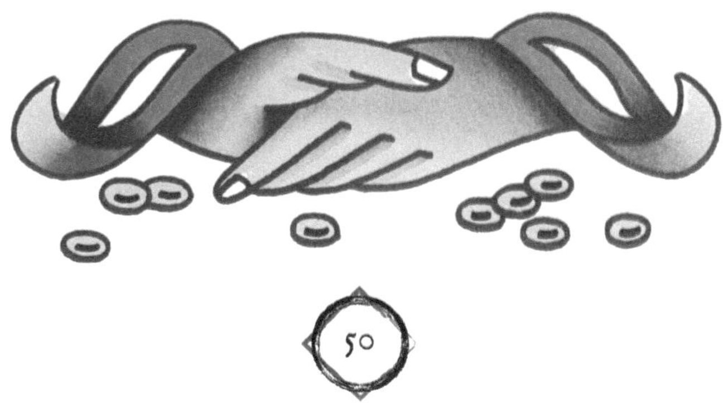

The gate shut behind the man as he made his way out of the kingdom. Jar of honey in hand, he looked down at it and smiled. He peered off into the distance to see JoAnn's farm in the light of day. On the horizon, a great winged figure flew towards him. The man waited intently, and the being landed before him sending dust in every direction.

Beautiful, white shimmering wings, and majestically robed with striking features; it was an angel. The man looked in awe at the angel, speechless for a moment.

Finally, the man asked the angel, "Who are you?"

The angel replied, "I am Death. Do you understand what I was trying to teach you?"

Paul and the Magic Sword

By: Ben Robertson

Once upon a time, a man named Paul lived a quiet life on his family's land. After his parents died in a tragic accident, he stayed with his sister Penelope and her family, working as a stable boy. His life was simple—mostly spent caring for the mules and horses, playing with his nephews, and dreaming of something more. He had no friends, and his only escape was the occasional glance at the beautiful Emelia, who lived near the village. One night, Paul was preparing a mule for his brother-in-law, Bran. Heading into town, Bran saw something strange: a trail of smoke rising from the great mountain.

The villagers avoided the mountain, fearing its eerie dangers, but Paul couldn't shake the feeling that something important was happening up there. Bran, always eager for adventure, made fun of Paul for never having a real adventure of his own. Bran's words stuck with Paul as he lay in the stables that night, thinking of a grander purpose for his life.

The next day, Bran returned from town, excited and holding a small sack of beans. He claimed an old mage had given them to him, promising that if planted, the beans could grow anything one's heart desired. However, the mage warned of side effects, including strange ailments and bizarre transformations. Bran was certain the beans were a gift, but Penelope was skeptical, worried that they had been tricked again, as they had in the past by other failed schemes.

That evening, Bran planted one of the beans. To everyone's amazement, by morning, a massive, magical tree had appeared, that produced many kinds of magical fruit. Excited, Bran and Penelope began planting more, hoping for a better future. But when Paul secretly took one of the beans for himself, he planted it deep in the forest, hoping for something far greater. As he watered it, the ground trembled, and something mysterious began to stir.

By the next morning, Paul discovered a sword—glowing with a strange power—had grown from the bean. As he marveled at it, he realized that the magic was real. There would, however, be consequences. His family was amazed by the magic; Paul remained uneasy. The mage had warned them: the price for magic was never easily seen. Paul realized that if he wanted to change his life, he'd have to prepare for the consequence and challenges head on.

With his new sword in hand, Paul made a decision. The beans had given them power, but they also carried risks. The true price wasn't just the magic, but the bravery needed to face the unknown. He meditated on the the Mage's warning: Could he be brave in the face of danger? Was he prepared for the unknown? even if it meant sacrificing something precious?

The village began to see the benefits of the magic—crops grew, water flowed in the river, and the abundance brought a return of hope. Paul knew that the magic wouldn't last long without sacrifice. He turned to his family and said, "We've been given a gift, but now we must face what it truly costs."

That night, the family gathered around the table, their lives changed by the magic. Paul stood up, determined. "I'm going to the mountain. There's more magic there, and we'll need it if we're to protect the village." Bran, Penelope, and the children agreed, knowing that while the road ahead would be fraught with dangers, there would yet be a glimmer of hope.

As Paul and Bran made their way up the mountain, the journey was grueling. The air grew thinner, and the path steeper. By the third day, they were exhausted, their hopes waning. But as the sun began to set on the fourth day, they reached the summit. There, amidst the swirling smoke and crackling flames, they saw something unimaginable—a massive cave, glowing with fire from within.

The fire was not from a bonfire or a camp, but from something far more powerful. As they approached, the ground trembled beneath their feet, and they heard the deep rumble of a creature stirring in the cave.

Bran grabbed Paul's arm. "That's no ordinary fire. This... this is a dragon."

Sure enough, as they drew closer, the silhouette of a great beast emerged from the shadows. The dragons scales shimmering like molten gold, unfurled massive wings and exhaled a plume of fire that lit up the night sky. But instead of attacking, the dragon simply watched them, its eyes gleaming with ancient wisdom. As they stood frozen, a voice echoed in their minds—its words both soothing and commanding.

"You seek magic, but not all that glitters is gold. To gain, you must give. Welcome to my feast."

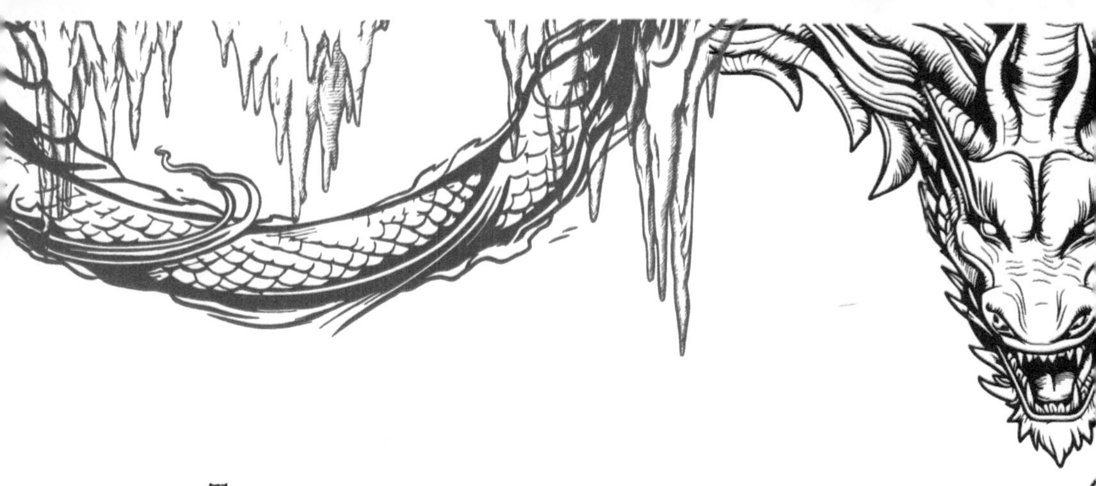

The dragon gestured with one claw, and before them appeared a magnificent spread: fruits, roasted meats, and steaming dishes of every kind. At the center of the table, a golden platter held a mountain of shimmering beans. The dragon spoke again. "These are the true beans of magic, born from the fire of my breath. They can fulfill your deepest desires, but they come at a price. Choose wisely, for everything you wish for must be paid for in equal measure."

Paul, overcome with awe, stepped forward. His thoughts turned to his family—how they had struggled, how they needed food, hope, and something to change their fortunes. He glanced at Bran, who seemed equally torn between desire and doubt.

"Can we take them? "Paul asked, his voice trembling.

"Yes," the dragon replied. "But remember, every wish made from these beans carries the weight of its cost. Choose wisely, or you will lose more than you gain."

With a mix of fear and anticipation, Paul and Bran each took a handful of beans, feeling their power hum in their palms. They looked at each other, knowing the choices they made would change their lives forever.

But before they could decide, the dragon spoke one last time, its voice softer now. "Feast first. Let the magic of the fire guide your hearts. Then, choose what you truly desire."

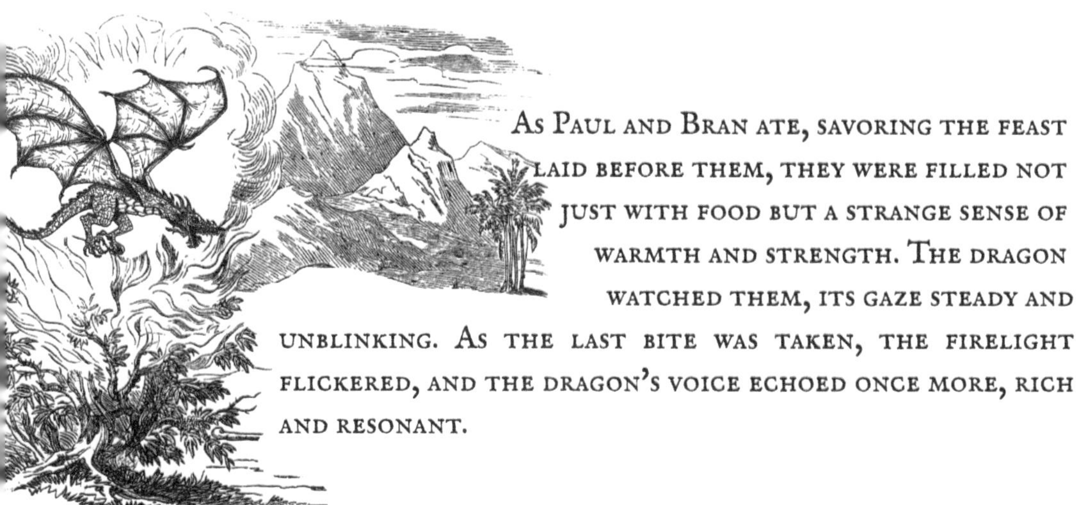

As Paul and Bran ate, savoring the feast laid before them, they were filled not just with food but a strange sense of warmth and strength. The dragon watched them, its gaze steady and unblinking. As the last bite was taken, the firelight flickered, and the dragon's voice echoed once more, rich and resonant.

"The price for feasting and taking the magic beans is simple, yet profound," the dragon intoned. "You must offer something of equal value to what you desire. It could be a piece of your past, a sacrifice of your future, or something you hold most dear."

Paul looked down at the glowing beans in his hand, a growing unease settling in his chest. Bran, equally uncertain, clutched his own handful of beans tightly. The promise of power, of a better life for their family, felt too good to resist. But the weight of the dragon's words hung heavily over them.

'But know this," the dragon continued. "The true cost is not measured by what you lose, but by how far you are willing to go to claim your wish."

Paul swallowed hard. He thought of his family—of his sister Penelope, of his nephews, of their struggles. He wanted to give them everything. But he also knew that taking the beans might come at a cost he could not yet understand.

Bran spoke first, his voice trembling with both excitement and fear. "I want our village to thrive again. I want to bring back the prosperity we've lost. I'll give whatever it takes."

The dragon's eyes glowed brighter as it acknowledged Bran's resolve. "Then take your wish, Bran. But know that you will not remain the same. Your bravery will be tested."

Bran took a deep breath, his hands shaking, and ate the beans. Instantly, he felt a surge of warmth fill his body, and in that moment, the dragon's fiery breath lit the sky. The land around them seemed to shift, as if the very mountain itself was responding to his wish. But as Bran looked around, a strange emptiness filled him. Something precious, something irreplaceable, was missing.

Paul, sensing his concern questioned, "Bran, what's wrong?"

Bran looked at him, his eyes clouded. "I... I don't know yet. But I feel... different. The magic has taken something, something I can't explain. Maybe my courage, maybe my heart. I don't know."

Paul turned to the dragon, fear in his eyes. "What price will I pay if I take my beans?"

The dragon regarded him for a long moment, its fiery eyes piercing through Paul's soul. "Your price, young one, will be one of great bravery."

"Bravery?" Paul asked, confused.

"Yes," the dragon said softly. "Bravery is not just in battle, but in choice. The price you will pay for your wish is the courage to face what lies ahead. If you want to bring change to your village, to your family, you must choose what you will stand for, even if it means standing alone."

Paul felt his heart race. He thought of his family, their hunger, their struggles. He thought of Emelia and the life he wished for, a life where he didn't just follow orders or hide in the shadows. He wanted to make a difference, to stand tall, to be seen as more than just the stable boy. He knew then what he had to do.

Paul stepped forward, holding the beans high. "I wish for the strength to change the world around me. To bring hope to my village. And to be the man I was always meant to be, no matter the cost."

The dragon nodded, approving his courage. "You have chosen wisely, Paul. You will be tested."

As Paul swallowed the beans, a rush of fire surged through him, and he felt his body fill with strength. The ground beneath him seemed to pulse with power. The mountain trembled, the sky darkened, and for a moment, Paul felt as though he could conquer anything.

Suddenly, the fire from the dragon's breath flared brighter, and a deep rumbling shook the earth. The dragon spread its wings wide, roaring into the night sky.

"You are ready," he said. "Go now, and face what comes."

Paul looked at Bran, who had regained his composure, and together they turned to leave the cave. The path down the mountain awaited them, but it was no longer just a way home—it was a journey that would shape their futures.

As Paul and Bran made their way down the mountain, the weight of their decisions lingered. The fire from the dragon's breath still flickered in their minds, and both of them knew the magic had already begun to take hold in ways they couldn't yet fully understand.

By the time they reached the village, the first light of dawn was breaking over the horizon. The air was crisp, the sky painted in soft hues of orange and purple. But as they approached the village gates, something felt different—there was a shift in the wind, a stirring that seemed to echo the change within them. Paul's heart raced with anticipation. Had they caused some sort of chaos? Did they bring down calamity with their choices? He wasn't sure what to expect, but he knew that something had changed deep within him.

When they arrived home, the village was eerily quiet. Penelope and the children were still inside, the usual sounds of daily life, absent. As they entered the house, Penelope looked up from the fire where she was cooking. Her eyes widened when she saw them, but what really caught her attention was the glint in Paul's eyes.

"Bran, Paul... what happened?" she asked, her voice tinged with worry.

Bran shook his head, a mixture of awe and uncertainty in his voice. "We... we met the dragon. We made a choice." Penelope was shaken "A dragon!" She fell back into a chair in disbelief. Paul stepped forward, holding out the sword that had grown from his bean—a weapon forged from magic and fire. "We didn't just find food, Penelope. We found power. The dragon gave us a gift, and we can use it to change things, to save this village!" His excitement was quickly tempered with concern. "He said... He said it may come at a cost."

Penelope's eyes darted between Paul and Bran, confusion and fear in her expression. "What do you mean, 'a cost'?"

Paul took a deep breath, his voice steady now. "I made a choice. The magic will give us strength, but we must be ready to fight for it. Against whatever comes our way." Bran nodded. "The dragon warned us. If we're to use the beans, we'll face tests we can't predict. But I believe the risk, the cost even, is worth it. I believe we can turn this around for all of us."

Penelope was silent for a long moment, her gaze drifting to the sword in Paul's hands. "And the dragon... you trusted him?"

Paul shook his head. "Well... I don't know. Nothing's free. The price of these gifts requires bravery, the price of bravery, sacrifice. Even if it costs us everything, I believe it may well be worth it."

The silence that followed was heavy with the weight of his words. Penelope stared at the sword, her thoughts churning. But then she sighed, her shoulders sagging in resignation. "I never thought I'd hear those words from you, Paul. You've always been... quiet, reserved, hidden. But now, you're standing here, ready to face the world. I'll follow you, brother. We'll fight together."

Paul smiled softly, grateful for her support and allegiance.

That night, as the family gathered around the table, Paul's thoughts wandered back to the mountain. The fire. The dragon. The future ahead. He knew that they would have to journey far beyond the village to make their wishes a reality. There would be more sacrifice, but at what cost? challenges than they could imagine. But one thing was certain: they would not be the same people who had left the village four days ago.

And it was then that the first sign of magic revealed itself.

As the family began to eat, a strange hum filled the air, and Paul felt a deep, pulsing energy around him. The beans, he realized, had already begun to take effect. The land outside began to stir—new growth sprouted from the earth, vibrant and green, as if the very soil was waking up from a long, deep sleep. The river, which had been dry for so long, began to trickle with fresh water, the sound of it flowing like a song of life returning to the land.

Bran stood at the window, staring out in disbelief. "It's working. The beans... they're bringing life back."

But even as they marveled at the magic unfolding before them, Paul couldn't shake the feeling that the real battle was just beginning. For the dragon had warned them: bravery was not just about facing the unknown—it was about standing tall in the face of danger, even when the odds seemed impossible.

And the mountain's fire was still burning.

The end?

The River in the Boy

By: Harrison Popham

Once upon a time there was a boy. This boy was born and raised where cold rivers cut through rolling wooded hills. Where the Hickory, Maples, Oaks, and Pops turn Scarlet, orange, yellow, and brown in the fall. Where the cedars and pines reach triumphantly to the heavens in the winter. Where the Summer displays every shade of green.
Where the woods come alive.

As a boy, he would escape to these woods for adventure and purpose. The boy loved many things, but he especially loved fishing the river with a dry fly in the summers and hunting in the brush in the fall and winters. When the world around him became so loud and overwhelming, he knew where he could escape for peace and serenity. The boy soon grew into a man and decided that there was nowhere else he'd rather be than in those woods. There was something about those woods that made him come alive.

So he set out to make a living in those very woods. In the spring and summer he would take people to the river in search of cold water trout, and in the fall and winter he took to the woods guiding people on the hunt for trophy Whitetail. He had spent so much time in this place as a boy and a young man, that it had become imprinted upon his soul. Hunting and fishing these lands became second nature. He was so skilled that his trips with patrons were almost always a success.

People began to talk about the boy from near and far. It became known all over that if you were visiting these Woods, he was the man to see. As time went on, the young man grew a small operation into five or six other young men gleaning from his expertise. They guided together all year long, and he taught them everything he learned over the years. He showed them all the richest locations and all the greatest techniques. The men all became successful outdoorsmen, yet not one of them were as graceful and successful as he was in those woods.

One summer day, the man took to the river on a scouting trip for an upcoming patron. His success in fishing had begun to slow down that time of year due to the summer heat, and he started to feel the weight of success. He took great pride in what he did, and he always did everything he could to ensure success for those for whom he was a guide. His upcoming patron was a returning customer. As a matter of fact, this man had booked so many trips with him that their relationship was more than business. A friendship.

That morning, the man woke up well before sunrise to give himself the best chance to beat the summer heat. He was on the water an hour before sunrise, and he patiently waited for first light. It wasn't a moment after first light broke when his fly was touching the water. He worked the stretches of the river he knew would produce first. He knew this river like a great musician knew his instrument. There wasn't a single spot of unfamiliar territory and nowhere he was unsure of. He had learned to make the river sing for him.

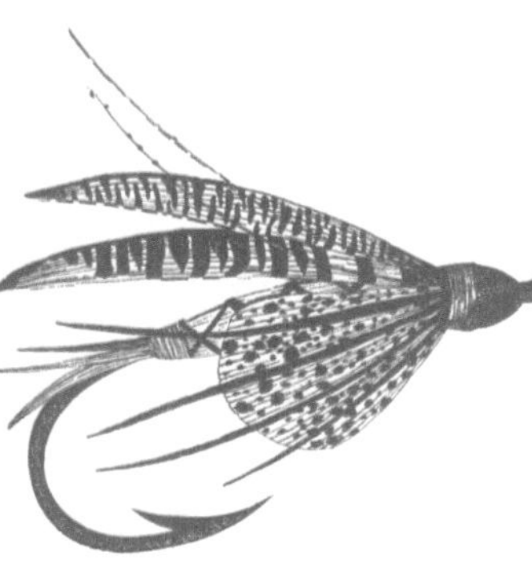

Knowing his chances were best early in the morning before the heat came, he fished hard. He fished for hours without even a rise. He started to work the water quicker in search of groups of fish holding in better water. Still, not even a rise.

His patience started to thin, and he started switching flies and doing everything that he knew. When even that wasn't working, he resorted to some of his best spots that he rarely would ever take anybody. When even those spots weren't producing, he started to become frustrated.

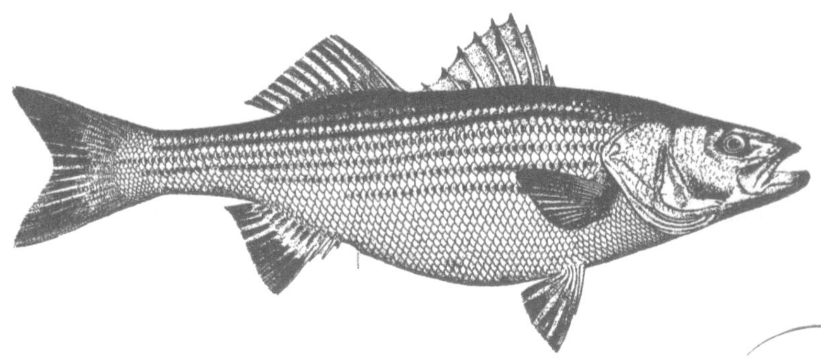

It was now mid-afternoon in the heat of the day and his chances of catching anything were slim to none. The older man began to break. His resolve was challenged; his confidence fleeting. He was making small mistakes over and over, and he began to be consumed by frustration. The same thing kept going through his mind.

"I must find something! This has never happened!"

His focus was hardly on fishing anymore. Frustrations rose and he began questioning himself in a detrimental spiral. He started working his way to a different section of river, and he was wading carelessly.

As he rushed through a swift section, the undercurrent ripped his left foot completely underneath him and spun him around. He lost all balance and was quickly washed away by the rapid water. He only floated down 30 ft or so before he could get his feet underneath him again. He gathered himself as best he could and made his way to the bank, where he angrily threw everything in his hands onto the ground.

He was now soaked and even more frustrated than ever. Full of defeat and embarrassment, even though nobody was there to see it, he made his way to a bridge just down river. He walked to the middle of the bridge and and sat down with his feet hanging over the water.

Looking out at the water in front of him, his anger and frustrations slowly made an exit. He gazed at the river in the woods that surrounded it. Before him were many memories. Memories of good days and bad. Memories of success and hardship. Memories of learning what was true and what was not. With all these memories flooding his mind, there was one thing that bothered him most of all. The thought of letting the very place he once came to escape the noise, becoming a place where the noise was allowed. He had invited this chaos into his secret place and his vocation turned into an occupation.

He made a decision from that day forward.
He would never again allow the "noise" in this place.
He would fiercely defend his secret place.

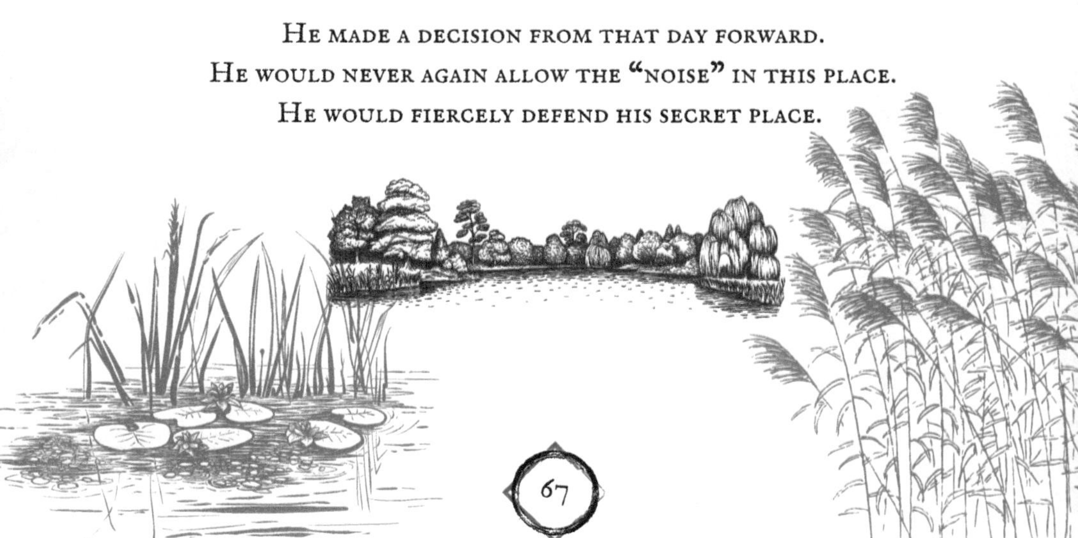

Herein Are

Stories Adapted From Foreign Tales

The Tables of Heaven and Hell

Adapted by: Peter Rye from a Chinese Proverb

Once upon a time, in a monastery built among the misty mountains of Greece, there lived two monks—one old, one young.

Having taken this young monk under his wing, the old priest modeled for the young monk how to pray, how to work, how to worship, and how to serve—both God and his brothers in the monastery.

One evening, at dinner just before Vespers, the young monk asked his older brother, "What are the differences between heaven and hell?"

"Well, that depends on whether we are talking about the heaven and hell in the age to come, or the hell on earth and the kingdom of heaven we can build now. The latter has much less material differences between the two," the wise monk said.

Puzzled, the young man asked, "What do you mean?"

"Take, for instance, this table. Both the kingdom of Heaven and hell, have a table in their dining halls. Right in the center of those tables are huge dishes of delicious foods, breads, and wines —the dishes giving off such appetizing aromas. And the amount of food is perfect for the amount of people seated around each of the tables."

"But strangely, both in heaven and hell, the diners have been given meter-long spoons and forks, chopsticks and tongs—and they have to use them to eat the food." The wise monk went on to describe, "and to eat, everyone must hold the utensils properly at their ends, no cheating is allowed, in either place."

"However, in the case of hell, everyone is starved because no matter how hard they try, they fail to get any of the food in their mouths using those utensils."

The young monk was still confused. "But Sir, wouldn't it be the same for the people in heaven?", he questioned again.

"In fact, no. In heaven, they can eat freely because all have learned to feed the person sitting opposite them at the table. You see, that's the difference between heaven and hell," smiled the older monk.

And with that, the last two monks at dinner cleared and cleaned off the table, and joined their brothers in the chapel for evening prayer.

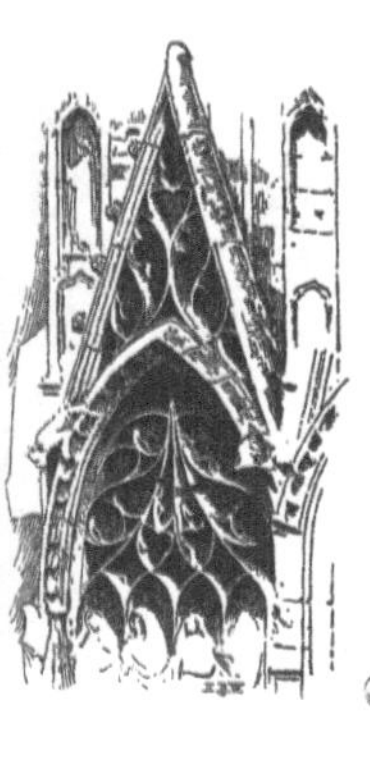

St. Ciaran and the Bell

from Irish Hagiography and Celtic Christian Wondertales

There once was a newly ordained priest in Ireland named Ciaran. Having just finished with the monks and bishop, Ciaran sets off to build an abbey that he will lead. He dreams that this church will house a congregation and students for divine worship. And just before he sets off across the green fields of Ireland to find a place suitable enough for his new church, a bell accompanies him—it begins to float right near him. St. Patrick has sent this bell and given it to Ciaran. This curious bell is set to ring whenever he has finally reached the place that God wants him to build the abbey.

So, Ciaran sets off. In comfort and ambition he goes to the most beautiful places the Emerald Isle has to offer. He goes to Dublin, to the Cliff of Mohr, and Galway, and still the bell doesn't ring. But he's certain that the bell should ring in the most beautiful of places. So, he heads to the other side of Ireland, thinking that maybe the bell will ring in the vast green fields—but, that means he will have to travel through the damp, dark, grotesque forest—filled with creatures and even dark magic. But, through the wood is the only way to reach the place he believes the bell will ring.

In the middle of the night, walking through that forsaken forest—
the bell rings. It is here that God wants him to build his church.
Embarrassed and confused, Ciaran dampens the sweet sound of the bell's ringing. Ciaran leaves immediately, escaping St. Patricks sound.
And just as he reaches the edge of the forest, the ringing stops...
Nowhere would the bell ring, but in that forest—in that forsaken, dark, grotesque, even pagan, place. And for some unknown, unforeseen reason, God wants a church there.

Reluctantly, and most unwillingly, Ciaran walks back into the wood, and he sets to building a cathedral in the thicket—an abbey in the undergrowth; and the bell begins to sing once again. Ciaran has obeyed and constructed his chapel.

But once the church has been completed, not a single human being shows up to his services. Raccoons, squirrels, mice, pigs, rabbits, owls—all the forrest dwelling creatures. These are his first congregants.
And Ciaran looks to God and asks, "why? Why are only animals coming to this church? Where are all the people? Why have you had me build this church in the middle of a forrest for only animals, God?"

Through time and service, Ciaran comes to realize that the story of Christianity transcends humanity—it goes to all levels of creation. Until Ciaran learns to love the earth, and pray for all its redemption and reconciliation— and not until then, will God bring the people he so desperately wants.

So, Ciaran obeys, reluctantly. He learns to love and serve his new congregants. And while his heart is changed in the process, slowly, people begin to arrive. Eventually, his abbey becomes all that he wanted it to be. The place of beauty that he'd imagined from the start —the forest has now been transformed into something teeming with life.

St. Peregrini and the Bees

from Irish Hagiography and Celtic Christian Wondertales

There once was a young man named Peregrini. For much of his life, he has strolled through the lush land of Ireland, leisurely enjoying his life. One day, however, Peregrini is walking along the coast - the seashore, and happens upon the body of the crucified Christ. Immediately he recognizes the wounds in his body and thinks to himself, "how could anyone have left the body of Jesus out here on the seashore like this?"

Rushing and determined, he hoists Christ up onto his shoulders and begins to carry Him.

He carries the body of the Lord for a long way, thinking that he must get the body back to a church or a holy site. But over time, Peregrini grows tired and weary. He begins to ache with the extra dead weight of Christ's body on him that he's been carrying for miles and miles.

And then, Peregrini falls into the sand, and falls asleep – worn out from the work of carrying Christ. When he has come to and wakes up, he realizes he's fallen. But now, terribly, the body of Christ has been stolen—it's no longer here. So he runs away, embarrassed that he lost Christ's body.

Peregrini holes up in the nearest pub and stays in their Inn for nearly a year until one day —a year to the day of when he dropped the body of Christ—an angel comes to him.

He asks him, "Peregrini, why are you hiding in here like this?"

Shocked, Peregrini responds, "Well, I'm embarrassed—
I haven't been able to talk to anyone about it.
But I have lost the body of Christ.
I was trying to carry it all the way here, but I failed."

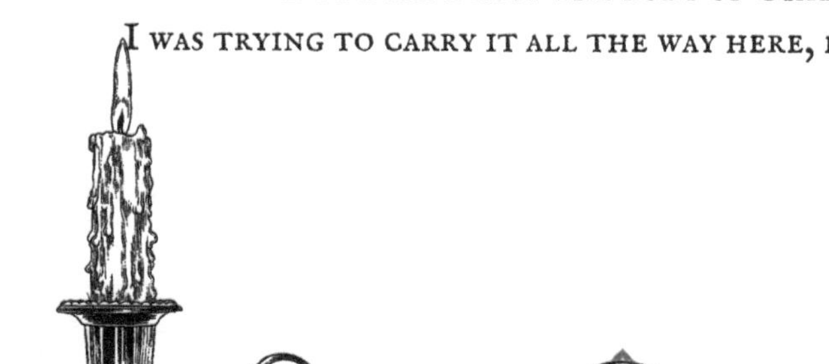

Here, the angel lets him in on a little secret, "No, Peregrini, that's not what happened at all. You see, when you fell—when you could no longer carry the weight of Christ's body—the bees flew from the hive, came and took His body to where they live. They've now built an entire chapel of honeycomb there. In fact, Peregrini, you have work to do. First, you do need to go and visit that chapel. But once you do this, your new vocation is to bring people on pilgrimage to this Bee Chapel—so that they too, may see, that where you fall, honey can be made."

So, Peregrini sets off in search of the chapel and sure enough, made of bright yellow comb and dripping honey, is this oddest of chapels, built right around the corner from where he fell and dropped Christ's body.

In this Bee Chapel, Peregrini stood amazed.
For the Eucharist, bread and wine were not served, but mead and honeycomb instead. There was not stained glass, but golden light filtering through the flowing honey. Something truly beautiful and unexpected had been constructed here. From then on, Peregrini took pilgrims from surrounding villages to visit the chapel—to come and see what had happened.

FIN

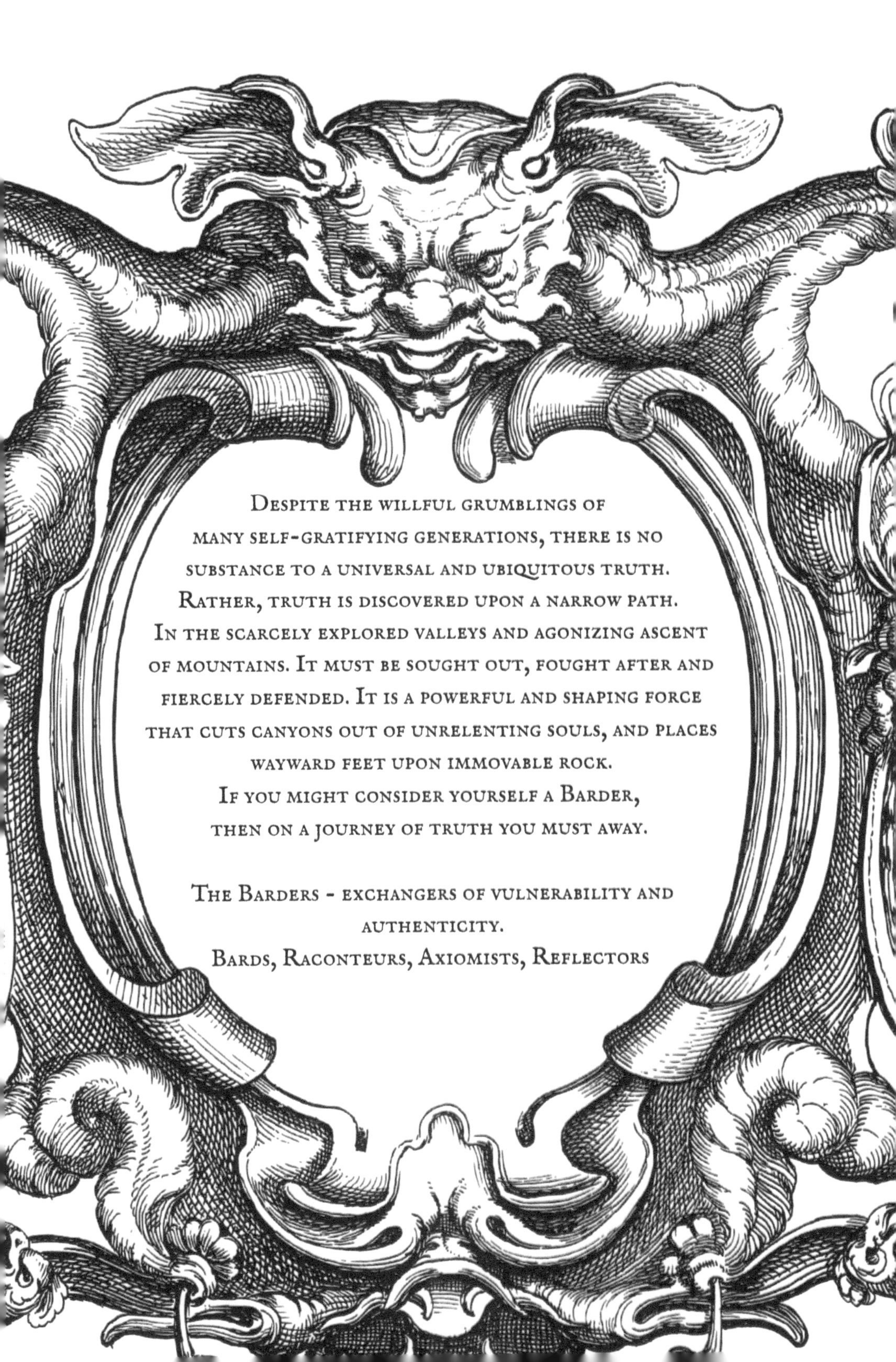

Despite the willful grumblings of
many self-gratifying generations, there is no
substance to a universal and ubiquitous truth.
Rather, truth is discovered upon a narrow path.
In the scarcely explored valleys and agonizing ascent
of mountains. It must be sought out, fought after and
fiercely defended. It is a powerful and shaping force
that cuts canyons out of unrelenting souls, and places
wayward feet upon immovable rock.
If you might consider yourself a Barder,
then on a journey of truth you must away.

The Barders - exchangers of vulnerability and
authenticity.
Bards, Raconteurs, Axiomists, Reflectors

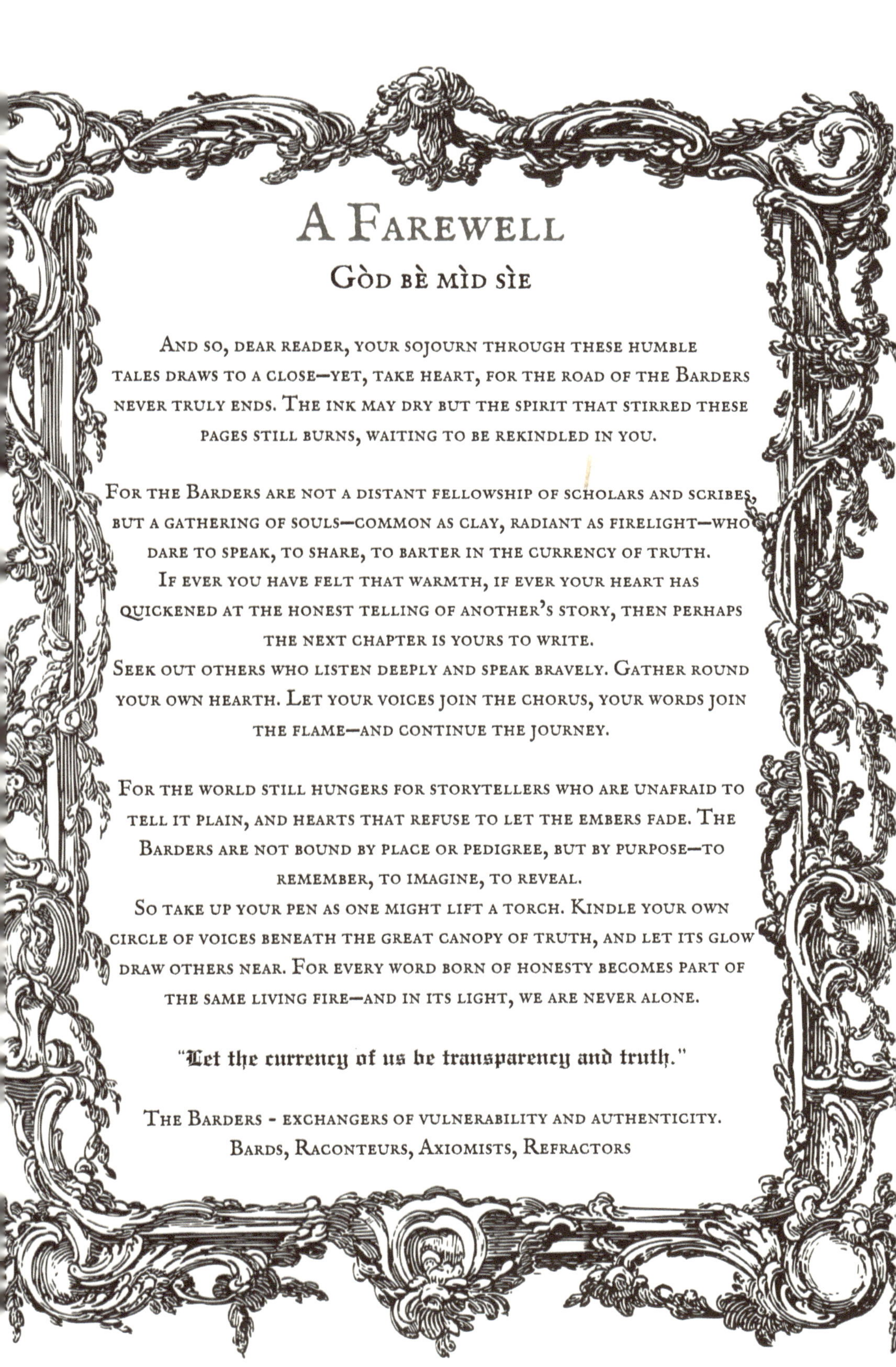

A Farewell

Gòd bè mìd sìe

And so, dear reader, your sojourn through these humble tales draws to a close—yet, take heart, for the road of the Barders never truly ends. The ink may dry but the spirit that stirred these pages still burns, waiting to be rekindled in you.

For the Barders are not a distant fellowship of scholars and scribes, but a gathering of souls—common as clay, radiant as firelight—who dare to speak, to share, to barter in the currency of truth.
If ever you have felt that warmth, if ever your heart has quickened at the honest telling of another's story, then perhaps the next chapter is yours to write.
Seek out others who listen deeply and speak bravely. Gather round your own hearth. Let your voices join the chorus, your words join the flame—and continue the journey.

For the world still hungers for storytellers who are unafraid to tell it plain, and hearts that refuse to let the embers fade. The Barders are not bound by place or pedigree, but by purpose—to remember, to imagine, to reveal.
So take up your pen as one might lift a torch. Kindle your own circle of voices beneath the great canopy of truth, and let its glow draw others near. For every word born of honesty becomes part of the same living fire—and in its light, we are never alone.

"Let the currency of us be transparency and truth."

The Barders - exchangers of vulnerability and authenticity.
Bards, Raconteurs, Axiomists, Refractors

www.ingramcontent.com/pod-product-compliance
Lightning Source LLC
Chambersburg PA
CBHW020743020826
48980CB00019B/772/J

* 9 7 9 8 9 9 3 9 0 2 2 1 0 *